Secret of the Tunnels

By Duane C. Burritt

*The Original Spider Club Mystery
for curious boys and girls ages 9-14*

Secret of the Tunnels

The Original Spider Club Mystery

By Duane C. Burritt

MOUNTZ
MEDIA & PUBLISHING

Illustrated by Darryl Washington

978-0-9840673-7-4
0-9840673-7-x
Secret of the Tunnels
The Original Spider Club Mystery

Published by Mountz Media & Publishing
P.O. Box 702398
Tulsa, Oklahoma 74170-2398
918-296-0995
www.mountzmedia.com

I dedicate this book to my wife, Linda, whose prayers and love helped me immeasurably.

Inspiration Behind The Spider Club Mysteries

When I was a boy in England in 1955, my family moved from Soham to a suburb near London, where there was an old shack in our backyard. My two friends from down the street, Johnny and Christina, helped me clean it up and make a clubhouse out of it. We decided to call our secret meeting place The Spider Club since we encountered more than our fair share of spiders there.

We spent many happy hours in the clubhouse eating meals and just talking about life. In fact, the clubhouse inspired me to write The Spider Club Mystery series to share my happy hours with a new generation of readers.

—**Duane C. Burritt**

CONTENTS

CHAPTER *1*

Ocean Crossing,
Trading Sun for Fog

It was 1954 and the dead of winter. There we were in the middle of
the Atlantic Ocean on our way from California to England in a huge ship

called the USS Patch. The sea roared and smashed into the sides of the ship, tossing it around like a toy boat. I do not recommend this to any traveler unless there is no other way.

The two upper decks were set aside for military dependents – in other words folks like my Mother, Mary; my sister, Nancy; and me.

I'm called William, but I prefer Will. I have Father's height or at least I will some day. I'm usually the tallest boy in my class, slender of build, but strong. My eyes are hazel, and I have blond hair.

Father, Henry Allen, had flown to England two weeks before to secure a place for us to live, so it was just the three of us on board the sick ship, as I called it. Everyone was sick except Mother, who was never sick, or at least so I thought. You couldn't go anywhere on the ship without seeing someone being seasick, which made me even more seasick.

The dining room, which I saw twice, was different from any place I'd ever seen before. The chairs were chained to the floor due to the waves rolling the ship side to side and back and forth; oh, just thinking about it makes me sick!

The tables had sides on them just like pool tables. Felt covered the tabletops, also just like pool tables. The plates had rubber on the bottom so they wouldn't slide off the table, but the food on the plates obeyed the laws of gravity, so the force of the waves tossed food all over the place even though we tried our best to keep it on the plates. I remember Nancy had a pork chop on her plate until we hit a big wave at which time it took up residence on the man's plate next to her plate. Glasses were filled half full so they wouldn't spill, and they had rubber on the bottom as well.

After two eventful meals in the dining hall, I decided to have my meals brought to my stateroom instead. I called it my stateroom, but really it was just a very small gray room with gray walls and gray beds; everything was painted Navy gray.

I'll spare you the details of our two weeks at sea, but let me just say I learned to live on saltine crackers and Pepsi. There was a porthole in the room but I didn't dare look out because the waves were so bad. If I've ever felt sicker I don't recall. I did venture out into the hallway once, but was glad to make it back to my room alive. You had to hold on to the rail and go hand over hand because if you let go you would certainly become part of the far wall.

We made port in Southampton, England, sometime in November. The weather was cold and damp, the sky was gray, and there was a heavy smell of smoke everywhere we turned. There was a sort of mist in the air and it was a little foggy. Later I learned this was one of the better winter days in England.

One of my first great adventures in England was riding in an English taxicab. It looked like a black box with doors. There was a line of cabs down the dock as far as I could see. All the same black boxes. Each one had a driver standing next to it, most of them talking to other cabbies. They all seemed dressed alike with funny-looking flat hats, wool or tweed sport coats, baggy slacks and black boots. Everything they wore was gray as far as I could tell.

Mother approached a driver and told him we wanted to go to Soham. We did not know where that was, but he seemed to know because he broke out in a large grin.

The cabbie began speaking to us, but we couldn't figure out what he was saying. Mother had told us that they spoke English in England, but so far we sure couldn't tell.

"Oie, mum, put your kit in the boot?" he kept asking.

We just stood there looking puzzled.

I looked at Mother and said, "I thought you said they spoke English in England."

"Yes, dear, they do," she responded.

"Then why can't we understand what he is saying?" I asked.

This went on for some time until the driver picked up our bags, put them in the trunk of the cab and opened the doors for us to get in, which we did.

The cab driver kept up quite a conversation on the journey to Soham, but we didn't understand what he was saying. Nancy and I kept quiet and Mother kept saying yes and nodding to whatever he said. I'm sure the cabbie had some story to tell his buddies later that night.

We lived in England quite some time before we found out that "Oie, mum" is a greeting to a mother, kit is luggage and boot is the trunk of the car. C'est la vie! (That's French for that's life, by the way.)

When we finally got to Soham, we realized why the cab driver was so excited to take us there. The trip took more than three hours and cost us a bunch of pounds sterling.

Driving into Soham was like stepping back in time or into a fairy tale. The streets were cobblestone and brick, all wet and dreary. The houses were the same drab brown as far as you could see. Some of the roofs were made of thick cut grass – thatching is what it's called. I always wondered why they didn't leak. The streets were narrow and curved back and forth, twisting like an old tree limb into the center of town. There were only a few buildings, maybe a half block long, but there were sidewalks and it seemed very clean.

We could smell the bakery before we could see it. The aroma of freshly baked bread filled the cab as we turned the corner onto the main street. I still see that street today when I smell fresh bread baking. Mr.

Moore, the baker, sold it by the loaf, not sliced, for about truppence, or three cents. Amazing. Then you could cut it as thick as you wanted, put it on a fork and hold it in the fire until it was toasted to your liking. A little strawberry jam and you had a treat like no other.

We came around a curve and before us stood the oldest looking church I'd ever seen. It had a high stone wall around it with glass sticking up on the top of it. I don't think they wanted anyone climbing over the wall. The tombstones surrounding the church were very old and gray, like everything else in Britain. They seemed to say, "Here I am but you can't read me because I'm too old," or "I'm leaning over so far you have to bend half over just to see what is written on me!"

Later we would explore that graveyard and see graves that were there long before the United States was even a glimmer in England's eye. The Rev. Holder was the vicar, or the head of the church, as we would learn later.

Along the side of the church was a driveway that seemed to enter a dark wood filled with trees that leaned over as if they were going to grab you as you came by. To a 9-year-old boy this was scary to say the least.

The drive curved to the right and then to left and then there it was: a very old house. Some of the places where windows should have been were bricked up. We later learned that this was done in England when a high tax was placed on glass.

Called St. Andrew's House, according to our landlord, the house used to be the vicarage for the church but now it was apartments. It was two stories tall with many rooms. There were several apartments and we were to live in one of them. The other apartments were vacant at the time.

The rooms had ceilings 12 feet high, and every room had a fireplace. This seemed strange to us until we discovered that there was no central heating. My room was a closet, so it didn't have a fireplace. Mother's solution for staying warm was to wear as many clothes as possible. I went to bed looking like an overstuffed turkey. There was one bare light bulb hanging from the ceiling in my room. In the corners were a collection of spiders of various sizes sitting on webs waiting for the light to go out so they could descend upon me in the middle of the night and chew on me with gigantic jaws. I slept under the covers.

My room was on the corner of the house facing the church bell tower. You can figure out how I awoke in each morning. I still hear those bells in my sleep sometimes. After two nights of freezing to death in our rooms Mother, to the great glee of Nancy and me, agreed to put her big bed in the living room right in front of the fireplace so we could all sleep cozy and warm together.

I don't know what you picture when I say fireplace, but the fireplaces in this house weren't the ones we know in America. In fact, the living room fireplace wasn't a fireplace at all; it was a huge cave in the living room wall. My whole family, including Father when he was home, could stand in it and have room left over.

On our first night in the apartment we were attempting to build a little fire in it when the caretaker, Tom Walsh, came up. He looked like an Iowa farmer dressed in coveralls, a thick brown jacket and Wellington boots. He was 6 feet or taller and about 250 pounds. He had short gray hair and a gray beard.

When he saw our little fire he laughed. "What in blazes is that?" he cried.

"Why, it's a fire!" Mother exclaimed.

"That's no fire for regular people, mum; it's a fire for the little people! Let me build you a proper fire, mum, so you and the young ones can be nice and warm," Mr. Walsh said.

"Sounds good to me," Mother quietly replied.

Mr. Walsh proceeded to build us "a proper fire." He brought in paper by the tons, armloads of twigs, then larger branches and finally he brought in tree trunks bigger than me!

"This here will give you a proper fire, mum, and be good and warm all through the night!"

I should think so since we seemed to have half the forest in our living room now. Not that it made any difference because our living room was so gigantic. We put the bed directly in front of the fireplace. The bed was flanked by our couch, a chair and a footstool. Besides the furniture facing the fireplace in a semicircle the rest of the room was empty. That's right, empty! We could have roller-skated in it if we were so inclined. But we were cozy by the big fire, sputtering and popping in blues, purples, reds, yellows, oranges and greens. It did indeed last all through the night and much of the next day as well.

So began our adventure in Soham, which would turn out to be one of the greatest adventures in my life. It's a time I've looked back on with great emotion and fear – a fear that visited me in nightmares for many years afterward.

Nancy was six years older than me and did not let me forget it. She was about 5 feet 5 inches tall with dirty blond hair and green eyes; I suppose by some standards she was pretty. She got straight A's in school and never studied that I could tell. She loved to dance and bought all the latest records. At the beginning of our Soham sojourn, we rode a bus to the military school, Lakenheath-Mildenhall.

The school was old with buildings made of metal, curved like a half circle. They were called Quonset buildings. They were built during World War II with no insulation; the only heat came from one pot-bellied stove in the middle of the classroom. The atmosphere was not conducive to studying, to say the least. There was a door at one end and the classroom was divided in half with a blackboard.

The blackboard could flip over from one side to the other, but mainly it was used to divide the class into grades. Third grade was on one side and fourth grade on the other. I was in fourth grade. My desk was against the wall, so that I had to bend over to do all my work. I was also quite far from the stove, so I had to keep my jacket on all the time.

I don't recall my teacher's name; I just remember that she was skinny like Popeye's girlfriend Olive Oyl. The little girl who sat in front of me had long red hair, which she wore in braids. I, of course, would pull them at every opportunity. Her name was Billy, which I thought was rather a strange name for a girl. She was short but spunky, and she could talk and talk and say nothing, but she was the prettiest girl in the fourth grade.

The desks were connected. My desk was attached to her seat and so forth. We used ink pens back then, so the desks had inkwells built into them. This provided the perfect opportunity for me to dip Billy's pigtails into my inkwell, which I did from time to time. She would complain to the teacher, and I would get yelled at. However, at recess I would chase her all over the playground until I caught her and stole a kiss. I guess she didn't mind because she always slowed down enough for me to catch her fairly easily. She was not the first girl I had liked – there was Michelle in kindergarten and Susan, the girl next door to us in California. But Billy was different, so I stole a kiss from her every chance I got.

Nancy decided that the military dependents school was beneath her dignity, so Mother enrolled her in an English convent school. Little did Nancy know that nuns teach in convent schools. Oh well, discipline she needed and discipline she got. She had to wear a uniform that consisted of a white blouse, a plaid skirt and a blue wool blazer complete with a golden crest on it shaped like a shield and a striped tie to top it off.

There was only enough money for Nancy to attend the private school, so I remained at the military school. The days were long and the ride on the bus was lonely for a 9-year-old boy. Mother would put my teddy bear, Freddy, up in my bedroom window so I could see him as I came up the drive after school. I always looked forward to that. Some might think I was too old for a teddy bear, but what could it hurt? So long as the guys at school didn't know.

Mother also would have a large slice of toasted bread with strawberry jam on it and a hot cup of chocolate waiting for me. Mother was about 5 feet 2 inches tall with short brown hair and dark brown eyes. She was petite and beautiful. She was very intelligent and a child prodigy. She began playing the violin at about age 4 and by 7 had totally amazed her tutor. By the time Mother was 12, she had played at Carnegie Hall in New York City. She sang in five different languages and performed onstage in all sorts of plays. Mother mostly raised us because Father lived on the base, where he was going to school or so we were told.

Our family was like every other American family in the '50s except for one thing – Father was gone most of the time. He was as tough as nails, having grown up on the streets of Chicago. He stood 6 feet 4 inches tall and was built something like a Mack truck. At age 12 he had to go to work in a steel factory to help his family. He gained strength by lifting steel ingots all day long for 14 cents an hour. At age 16 he returned to high school, and when he was 17 he became the Illinois state high school wrestling champion. He joined the National Guard when he was 18 and started college.

World War II began and his guard unit was activated before he could finish college. He served with distinction in World War II and the Korean War, winning many medals, including four Purple Hearts and the Silver Star. When the United States Air Force started, he transferred from the Army Air Corps and joined the Air Force pistol team.

For a boy of 9 it was hard to have an absentee Father, especially when there were balls to catch, bats to swing, bikes to ride and no one to teach me these things.

If Mother was athletic when she was young, I never knew it; Nancy never swung a bat in her life, or at least that's the way she looked whenever I tried to get her to play with me.

Being 15, Nancy was beginning to think of other things besides sports, namely boys. She did play field hockey at the convent school, though, so I can't say she was a total sports dud.

Nancy and I were blessed twice a month with a small allowance. She got one pound, and I got 10 schillings, or about $1.40. That doesn't sound like much, but it really was quite good for those times. I did OK and when I needed more cash I would just go to Mother, who always had a little extra for her "good little boy."

Things were cheap in England in the '50s. For example, you could get a small bag of candy for a farthing, or about one fourth of a cent. Miss Stone, the candy storeowner, was always kind to me and let me sample the candy. She was a skinny spinster with mousy brown hair. Her face seemed drawn in, and she had high cheek bones. Her Adam's apple bobbed up and down when she talked.

Her love was her dogs. They were Corgis, the small breed the queen favored. Miss Stone had four of them. She always had some new kind of candy, and I always had to try it.

Saturday was a special day because Mother would go shopping on the base, Lakenheath-Mildenhall, and leave Nancy and me at the base theater. For 25 cents you could get into the movie and get a large bag of popcorn. Five or six cartoons preceded the main feature, which was usually "Jungle Jim," "Flash Gordon" or a western.

However, the theater would show just part of the movie – stopping it at some cliff-hanging point. You had to come back the following Saturday to find out how it ended.

Those were great times, and I have fond memories of those days, especially when Father would come home. Father was basically a good man. He was troubled by problems we knew nothing about until years later. He provided everything we could possibly need if it was within his power.

Father was something of a scrounger, really. He would show up at home with the strangest things. Once he came home just before Christmas with a ton of wrapping paper, all green. I don't know how much there was, but we had presents wrapped with green paper for years after that.

Another time he came home with a case of canned meat – 144 cans. We cooked this meat every way you could think of for a long time. It was many years before I could even look at a can of that stuff.

Mother would ask, "Honey, where did you get that?"

He would reply, "Oh I just picked it up from a friend," or "Some guy was going back to the states and couldn't take it with him."

On the Saturdays when Father came home, he'd have a little nap and then we would hop on the train and head into London for dinner and a movie.

Dinner out as a family was always something special to me. We found a little Chinese restaurant in an alley just off Piccadilly Circle. It looked like a dump, but the food was fantastic. The first time we went in we asked for menus, but the man just kept saying, "No, no, you see, me fix, you see!"

He came back with all sorts of goodies, each dish on a separate metal platter complete with a top. Each container was small but there was always enough, actually more than enough. We stuffed ourselves on fried rice, plain rice, cashew chicken, sweet and sour pork, wonton soup, noodles, chow mien. There was hot tea of many different flavors and fortune cookies. What kid doesn't love fortune cookies?

An Indian restaurant on Swallow Street in London also was a favorite of ours. I remember this huge man with a black beard wearing a red turban, a red vest and a gold sash around his waist. He was as tall as a mountain, and he slowly walked us to our table and held out Mother's chair for her to sit down. Everything there was spicy, but we got used to it. The curried rice was my favorite.

Once we tried a new place because it advertised American hamburgers. Just the thought of an American hamburger was too much to pass up. We almost got sick with our first bite. The chef had taken the meat, seared it quickly on both sides and slapped it on a bun. It was basically raw meat. We took the burgers back to the kitchen and Mother proceeded to explain how to properly cook a hamburger. The owner, instead of getting mad, was quite pleased to have an American tell him the right way to make a burger, so he cooked them again and they were great. We returned many times.

Once we went into London to see Queen Elizabeth II's birthday celebration. At that time she had been queen for about only two years. It was a wonderful day: There were parades and bands and the queen rode in a golden coach pulled by eight beautiful white horses. The Queen's Guard preceded her wearing silver helmets with long plumes protruding from the top. Their long, black riding boots gleamed like glass.

Behind the band came the Grenadier Guards. These are the guards who stand in front of Buckingham Palace. They don't move or react – no matter what kind of face people make at them. I know; I tried it!

The guards are all very tall decked out in their red coats and black pants with a red stripe along the side. The hats are the most impressive part of their uniform. They look like they're made from bear fur and are very high with a strap that fits between the guards' lips and chin.

The weather in England was usually terrible, except in July and August. The rest of the year was either cold or rainy or both. We had fog as thick as mud and snow as deep as any we experienced in Virginia.

Most of my relatives lived in Hampton Roads, Virginia, and worked in the shipyards.

When Father returned home from World War II he got a job as salesman. While I don't know what he sold, I believe he must not have liked selling it because he quit. Mother said Father quit because he wasn't paid for what he sold. So Mother had to get a job at the local electric company.

Father kind of drifted from job to job; I guess we were considered poor by most folks.

When I was 5 years old I remember Father packing a large, green canvas bag. He wore a blue uniform that I had never seen before.

"Where are you going Father?" I asked.

"Korea," he said.

"Where's Korea?" I asked.

"Far away son, far away," he replied.

I didn't see Father for a long time after that. When he finally returned he said we were moving to California, where it was sunny and nice. Our destination? The March Air Force Base in Riverside, California.

That's where Father was stationed after the Korean War. He put in for housing on the base, but there wasn't enough so we had to buy a trailer and live off the base. I'll never forget when they moved our trailer into the trailer park lot.

Father, wanting us to have the best trailer he could find, bought the largest one they made at that time, or so he told us. It was a whopping 45 feet long and 10 feet wide! The whole trailer park neighborhood came out to see it. We were so proud. It took some work to get it positioned right.

Our trailer had a canvas awning of green and yellow stripes that extended over the patio; we were the talk of the trailer park. We finally sold our trailer and moved onto the base when a house became available. It was from there we moved to England in the winter of 1954.

It was quite a shock moving from sunny California to freezing England, but we soon adjusted, or at least we tried to adjust. I don't think I've ever been as cold as when we lived in England. It was damp all the time, and the cold wind seemed to shoot through you like an arrow made of ice.

And the fog, well you've never seen real fog until you've lived in England. London is famous for its air pollution and when mixed with fog it could be down right dangerous.

One time we were in London during a bad fog. All of a sudden it turned blacker than dirt. We couldn't even see our feet. Mother, Nancy and I were together. Mother grabbed our hands and we carefully, and very slowly, felt our way from the street across the sidewalk to a storefront. We edged along the wall until we felt a doorknob and we went in. To our surprise it was an old-fashioned English tea room.

As soon as we entered someone yelled, "Close that door!"

You could see the fog seeping under the door. It was creepy. We found out later from the BBC news that the fog had descended on London, combined with the air pollution and produced what they referred to for years as the Killer Fog. Its density made visibility impossible, causing accidents in which many people were killed and injured. It was the worst fog to hit London since records were kept. The fog eventually lifted, and we made it back to Soham.

Soham is near two other small towns: Ely and Newmarket. Newmarket was famous at that time for horse racing.

Soham was like a picture postcard for England with its thatched roofs and quaint little shops. Mr. Thatcher owned the butcher shop. He stood about 5 feet 5 inches tall and was heavy set with large thick hands. He had a deep voice and always seemed to be grumpy, but he was decent to us probably because we spent more money than anyone else who came into his store.

Mr. Thatcher always wore a white coat that was always covered with blood and looked like it never had been washed. He killed and dressed his animals right behind his shop. The floor was covered with sawdust and blood. We often heard pigs squealing.

When we first went to the butcher shop Mother was stunned to find meat hanging in front of the store, complete with flies. Mother was used to clean and neat stores in the United States. She decided not to purchase anything from his shop, but then changed her mind. After all, we had to eat. And cooking the meat killed the germs.

The first time we got the courage to buy something from Mr. Thatcher, Mother ordered six pork chops.

"Oh, mum, what would you be wanting with six pork chops?" asked Mr. Thatcher.

"Why to cook, of course," Mother said.

"Good, oh mum, you must have a big family then, right?" he asked.

"No, just the three of us," said Mother.

"Right mum, if it's six pork chops you want, it's six pork chops you'll get," he replied.

After that he loved to see us coming.

The item we loved the most from the butcher shop was the pork sausage. Mr. Thatcher made the sausage himself and was very proud of it. When you cooked the sausages the skin split open and the smell perfumed the house.

Like many things in England, grocery shopping was a different experience. Most folks shopped every day because they didn't have iceboxes or refrigerators. There was no going to the store and stocking up for a week like in the United States. We eventually got an icebox but until then we shopped every day and had fun doing it.

Our favorite shop was the bakery. Mr. and Mrs. Moore owned it. Mr. Moore was very fat, stood about 5 feet 5 inches and had a red round face. He must have weighed more than 300 pounds. Mrs. Moore was about 5 feet tall and also very fat. A cheerful woman, she always wore an apron and reminded me of my grandmother.

The bakery's wares were displayed in glass cases so you could see all the delicious pastries and pies: cherry, apple, coconut cream, lemon meringue, mince, strawberry and many more. The Moores also made little tarts with cream fillings, coffeecakes and dozens of pastries. Fresh bread and cookies of all kinds that melted in your mouth were part of the equation too. My favorite were the petit fours – small pastries made of cake with several layers of frosting or jelly between each layer encased in a harder, sweeter frosting. Mrs. Moore called them tea cakes.

Specialty shops made up the rest of Soham, including a tailor shop and a small general store that doubled as a post office. I loved this store more than any other place because Mrs. Wallis, the owner, sold toys there. She looked like a schoolteacher I used to have with her gray hair tied up in a bun. She was tall and slim, maybe 5 feet 9 inches. If she ate anything it didn't show. Her eyes were light blue, and she always wore the same style of gray or blue dress that went straight to the floor, or almost. She also wore a little blue vest that had a British mail badge on it since she doubled as the postmistress. The post office consisted of a small counter in the back of the store covered by wire with a little window in it.

The toys Mrs. Wallis sold were great. She stocked wind-up race cars, rubber farm animals and English knights, the best toys you could buy in my opinion.. Hand made of metal and hand painted, the knights were expensive – at least on my allowance. Most of my collection came as Christmas presents.

My knights were an escape for me. When I played with them I could slip into my imagination and get lost for hours. Later I would need them very much. I also collected marbles and comic books – the usual stuff young boys collect.

We loved to order fish and chips from the local fish vendor. He stood 6 feet 3 inches with black hair and a large scar running down the left side of his face. He never said much, just took our order and then filled it. His accent didn't seem British to me and Mother commented on it once, but we never gave it another thought.

The fish vendor had a small lean-to behind the post office where he sold his fish and chips. It was just a small wooden shed with one counter. It couldn't have been more than 6 feet wide at the most. You could hear the fish frying in the bubbling hot oil. They were the best I've had anywhere. For about $1.40 you got about six large pieces of fish and more chips (french fries) than you could possibly eat. He wrapped it all up in newspaper and Mother would put our meal in her large shopping bag and home we went as quickly as possible to eat our feast before it got cold.

Sitting by the huge fireplace eating fish and chips on a cold night and sipping hot chocolate, it didn't get any better than that. Except for the cold and snow, everything in our world was as it should be. We didn't know that our seemingly idyllic life was about to change.

CHAPTER 2

Into the Tunnels

Our Soham apartment consisted of several rooms in a home that was more like a castle than a house. The front doors at the main entrance were solid oak about 12 feet high. They were rounded at the top and carved with beautiful patterns. The hinges alone were more than a foot long; no telling how much they weighed.

The handyman Mr. Walsh, or Tom as he preferred to be called except when Mother was around, told us we could tour the oldest part of the home if we liked. When we first arrived, the house was vacant except for us and Tom and his wife, so touring it didn't disturb any other tenants.

We looked at the original kitchen first. It was huge, the biggest kitchen I'd ever seen. The ceiling was higher than the rest of the house, maybe 20 feet high. The table was suspended overhead, hanging from the ceiling by ropes and pulleys. Tom said they kept the table up when the kitchen was not in use because it was easier to clean the floor and the abundant counter space rendered the table unnecessary unless they were preparing for a big event like a banquet.

Six ovens made of stone with brick lining were the centerpiece of the kitchen. They had imposing iron doors and were about 10 feet deep. I noticed long paddles that looked like boat oars; Tom said they were used to put bread and other items deep into the ovens. They sure could bake a lot of bread in those! Wood, and later coal, fueled the fires that heated the ovens. There were also several small fireplaces with iron hangers for hanging pots to simmer stews and such.

We explored every nook and cranny of the house, discovering spiders – much to my dismay – at every turn. I hate spiders with a passion and have a deathly fear of them. Father did not understand this. He figured that you overcame a fear by doing what you feared most.

So, for example, when he found out I could not swim Father remedied that by picking me up by the back of my belt and the collar of my shirt and throwing me, clothes and all, into a fast-flowing canal.

"Time you learned how to swim, boy," he said as I landed in the freezing water.

I was quickly pulled to the bottom and got stuck on a metal gate. Father had to jump in to save me.

Mother would not let him hear the last of that little caper for a long time.

"What on God's green Earth were you thinking, Henry?" she asked. Mother always called Father Henry when she was mad at him.

All he could do was respond with his standard answer to any situation in which I ended up crying.

"Stop crying; real men don't cry," he'd shout.

I kept crying, and he'd stomp off mumbling under his breath.

And so it was with spiders. Father tried to get me to hold one, or touch one, and I didn't want to touch a spider any more than I did a skunk!

Father persisted until one day he locked me in the coal bin and said I could not come out until the coal bucket was full. Keeping the coal bucket full for Mother's stove was one of my chores. When Father wasn't home I could get Mother to do it, but if he was around I had to do it.

It wasn't so bad when the coal bin was full, but as the coal got lower and lower, I had to reach farther into the shed to get at the coal. And the shed was full of spiders, lurking in the shadows just waiting to attack me if I ventured too close.

One day I had to get the coal and it was way out of my reach. I stepped into the shed, or coal bin as we called it, and was about to shovel some coal when Father snuck up behind me, shut the door and locked it.

Suddenly it was pitch black and I screamed!

Father was unsympathetic.

"You can come out when the coal bucket is full and not until," he said.

I panicked. I could picture those spiders beginning to make their way toward me, jaws dripping with poison and big hairy legs ready to jump on me.

"Help!" I cried.

Eventually Mother came to my rescue and Father was in the dog house for a week after that.

Looking back on those days, I don't think Father meant to be mean. He was just trying to make a man out of me. I just don't think he went about it the right way.

But back to exploring the grand home in which we lived. The most exciting thing happened one day when Tom was outside shooting at crows.

"They are always getting into the Missus' garden," he said, grumpily. "I shoot up in the tree tops and they fly off, well, at least for a time anyway."

"William, my lad," he continued. "I haven't shown you the tunnels, have I?"

"What tunnels?" I asked with excitement.

"Why, the tunnels under the house, my lad, the tunnels under the house. They go all over the place, some for several miles," Tom replied.

"Are you sure?" I asked.

"As sure as I'm standing here looking at you," Tom said.

"Why would anyone want a tunnel that long?" I thought out loud.

"For escaping, for getting away from bad people who are trying to get you," Tom answered.

"Getting away from who, what bad people?" I asked.

"Well, you see, my lad, this here house used to belong to a very important man long ago; he was in the English government and built these tunnels under his house so if he needed to, he could escape to another town," Tom explained.

"Wow!" I said. "Can I see 'em?"

"You better ask your mum, lad, and see what she says," Tom replied.

"I'll do it right now, Mr. Walsh, just wait. I'll be right back," I replied.

So off I went to tell Mother about the tunnels under the house. She didn't share my enthusiasm.

"Oh, no, dear, I don't think you ought to be going down into any tunnels. They might not be safe!" she said.

That's just what I expected her to say; so I begged and begged until she agreed for all of us to have just a little look, but "not too far in."

That was good enough for me, and so Mother, Nancy and I went with Mr. Walsh into the basement, where we came to a big door. Mr. Walsh said he kept it locked because it was the entrance to the tunnels.

When he opened the door, a powerful musty smell assaulted our nostrils. The first thing we saw when we entered was a huge spider web across the path. That was enough for me, but Mr. Walsh brushed it aside and said it was all right; so I clung tight to Mother, with Nancy hanging on her other side (she had no great love for spiders either).

Mother could sense our fear and said, "I think we've seen enough, Mr. Walsh. We'll be going back now."

"But, mum, we just got started. There is so much more to see," he said.

"I think we'll wait until my husband is here before we do any more exploring, thank you," Mother said with authority.

So we turned around and went back upstairs. Even though my fear of spiders was almost overpowering, my curiosity about the tunnels was more so. I decided to bide my time. I knew there would be another day in the tunnels and another and another!

School in England wasn't much different than school in America. Times tables and spelling words ruled my life. If I missed a word on my spelling test on Friday Mother would make me write the word 100 times. If you have to write a word 100 times, you remember how to spell it.

School was OK if you liked freezing while you worked, but recess made up for all my trials in the classroom. Since it was winter we had our share of snow.

One day all the kids decided to make a snowman, so we began rolling the first snowball that was to be the base of the snowman. We got carried away, though. We kept pushing it and pushing it until it wouldn't move anymore. We needed help. A cry went out across the playground and more kids showed up. We now had power to move the great snowball anywhere, so we pushed and shoved and yelled and grunted.

We pushed it as far as we could and came to a stop to admire our efforts. Our snowball had to be the biggest in the world! It was 8 or 9 feet tall and contained all the snow (and some grass) from the playground.

Now the only problems were how to get a second snowball up there and where would to get the snow. We had created a monster. It became apparent that the first one to the top of this snowball was going to be king of the playground. I knew it was going to be me, but everyone else had the same idea at the same time and the fight was on. I tried to get a foothold, but every time I did someone would knock me down and step on me trying to get to the top.

After several attempts at snow mountain climbing I realized that I was not going to get to the top unless I had some help. I decided that climbing up on someone else would work if I was careful and they didn't fall in the process. After some time and exertion, I finally made it to the top only to get knocked down again.

I was not daunted because I was a Virginian, and Virginians are tough! On and on I climbed, just to be knocked down again and again. Then the whistle blew. Recess was over.

As we proudly walked back to the building, Billy came running over and said softly, "Oh, William, you were so brave."

At first I thought she was making fun of me and then I realized she was serious. Oh, no, did this mean what I thought it did?

Yes, it did. According to Billy, we were going steady. Do you know what this means to a fourth-grader? It means life as you know it is over. The other guys would tease me until I couldn't stand it any longer. What would Mother say? Why did I chase after Billy and kiss her? How stupid could I be! I had lost my freedom. I was a fourth-grader with no future. I was doomed to join the ranks of what Nancy called the steady teddies.

Good grief, how could this have happened? I liked Billy, but now the thrill of the chase was over and I felt betrayed, grounded, doomed to going through elementary school with Billy constantly at my side.

Did this mean we were engaged? I've heard of that and that usually meant you got married next. I remember seeing a movie in which a redhead yelled at her husband and had a horrible temper. Billy was a redhead. Maybe I could join the Foreign Legion. No, I was too young. What was I going to do?

Then the answer occurred to me. The Air Force would save me. Why didn't I think of that earlier? Father was rarely stationed anywhere for more than three years. That was it. I'd move sooner or later and that would be the end of it, unless Billy's Father was transferred to the same base. No, that would never happen.

Those were my school day dramas. At night I'd dream of going back into the tunnels. I wondered what was lurking down there just a few feet below my bedroom. How long were the tunnels? Was there really one several miles long?

Maybe Father would be home soon and we'd find out. Mr. Walsh had the keys to the basement and the tunnel door, and I knew where he kept them. I don't think he knew that I knew he put them in the kitchen pantry, or at least he didn't show it.

What if I could sneak down there at night, when everyone was asleep, get the keys, go to the basement, into the tunnels and explore them by myself?

No, I guess I'd be too afraid to do that, but I could imagine doing it. I'd creep down the stairs, go into the old kitchen, get the keys and open the door to the basement. With my trusty Boy Scout flashlight I could see well. I wasn't a Boy Scout, but Father had bought me a Scout flashlight anyway because they were dependable.

In my fantasy, as I looked down the basement stairs I remembered that the first stair creaked loudly, so I had to skip that stair and go directly to the second stair, taking care not to fall or make any noise.

The basement was dark, eerie and damp. Everything smelled musty. It was cold in the basement, so I wore a jacket. Now I had to be brave. Look out spiders, here I come.

Now I was at the solid oak door that barred entry to the tunnels. The key was bigger than any key I'd ever seen. It must have weighed a pound. As I turned the key and the door opened, my nostrils were filled with that damp, musty odor that I'd smelled before. Cold air rushed at me as though someone had put a fan in the tunnel. It was pitch black, but my trusty Boy Scout flashlight guided the way.

Wait. What if the door closed behind me and I couldn't get out? A chair, that's it! A chair from the basement could keep the door propped open. There was a lot of old furniture in the basement. That would do it. I could see the walls of the tunnel. They were shiny and slimy looking, like they were wet.

Terrible dark shapes lurked around every corner, but I was not afraid. I just kept going.

"William, William."

What's that? A voice. It sounds like Mother. Oh no!

"William, get up it's time to get ready for school," the voice said.

It was Mother, rousing me from my dream.

We went to town most every day. It was a cold walk and often snowy, but since it was not far from our home we didn't mind. I made a point of visiting with each store clerk and telling them about the tunnels, but they all seemed to know about them.

It seemed to be no big deal to them since they knew all the local history. Mr. Thatcher, the butcher, said he had been inside the tunnels once.

"How come?" I asked.

"Well, William, I'll tell you. I tried to buy that house you live in, but the vicar, Rev. Holder, wouldn't sell it," he said grudgingly.

"But I thought Mr. Styles owned it," I said.

"No, my lad, Mr. Styles is the landlord, but actually the church owns the property and Rev. Holder is the vicar of the church, so what he says goes. Anyway I offered him a fair price for it, but he said renters like yourself provide enough funds to keep it up and pay the taxes on it."

"So how did you see the tunnels?" I asked.

"Rev. Holder took some of the townspeople on a tour of the home and the tunnels a couple of years ago. The whole town was having celebrations and parties because of the queen's coronation."

"What's a coronation?" I asked.

"It's when a man becomes king or a woman becomes queen, in this case it was a queen, Queen Elizabeth II. Anyway the whole town was celebrating and Rev. Holder gave tours of the house," he said.

"So who went on the tour with you, Mr. Thatcher?" I asked.

"Well, there was Mr. and Mrs. Moore, Mrs. Wallis, Miss Stone, some other townsfolk and myself. I remember vividly the occasion because Miss Stone seemed hesitant to go, but we talked her into it, and also she was very afraid of the skeletons."

"What skeletons?" I queried.

"There are skeletons down there still attached to chains on the walls where they were left to die," he replied.

"You're kidding!" I exclaimed.

"No, lad, they're really there, and no one knows what lays beyond the door to the long tunnel," Mr. Thatcher said.

"So there really is a long tunnel all the way to another town?" I asked with surprise.

"Maybe lad; know one knows for sure. Mr. Styles keeps it locked so no one can get trapped in there. For all we know it has collapsed somewhere along the way and it could be dangerous. Sorry to go lad, but I have a turkey to kill for a customer. Enjoyed talking with you lad," Mr. Thatcher said.

"Yes, sir, I enjoyed talking with you, too. Bye!"

And off we went to the post office while I mulled over my conversation with Mr. Thatcher. The post office was just down the main street and around the corner from the butcher's shop.

I enjoyed walking through town because you met all sorts of local people and they always nodded but wouldn't say much. They didn't seem to be that friendly, really, but Mother said it was just the way English people were and not to worry about it; so I didn't. I tried to be friendly by smiling at people. I discovered if you smile at people they usually smile back.

I loved to go to the post office because of all the toys Mrs. Wallis had there. Mrs. Wallis was thinking of moving to America to live with her sister in Florida, so she would always ask us about Florida whenever we came in. I guess she figured that since we were Americans we would know all about Florida even if we had never lived there.

Mother was in Fort Meyers once to meet Father during the war, but I was never there. I wasn't even a thought in their mind at that time, or Nancy either. Mother told Mrs. Wallis that Fort Meyers had beautiful beaches with lots of palm trees. Mrs. Wallis' sister lived in the panhandle of Florida in a small town called Milton, and we had never heard of it. She showed us pictures of her sister's house, but all we could see were pine trees.

"That sure doesn't look like Florida," I said.

Mother said it looked more like Virginia than Florida.

Anyway, Mrs. Wallis said there were too many memories for her in Soham and as soon as she could raise the money she was off to America. I felt sorry for Mrs. Wallis, having lost her husband and all. She never mentioned any children, so I guess she didn't have any.

One of my other favorite places to go in town was the candy store. Mother had a serious sweet tooth, so that really helped! Candy was inexpensive too. For two or three cents you could get a whole bag of the best chocolate I've ever eaten. The shop had white chocolate, chocolate swirls, licorice and every kind of candy you could think of. Miss Stone, the candy shop proprietor, wasn't married but I heard her tell Mother that she had been engaged once and it didn't work out. She said her fiancée had left her at the altar. When I asked Mother what that meant, she told me I'd understand when I got older. I hated it when Mother told me that. It was the standard response I got when she didn't want me to know the answer to something.

There was one man in town that I could never get to say much. In fact, we didn't even know his name at first. He sold the fish and chips in the little stand behind the post office. I tried to talk to him, but he kept quiet. He took your order, filled it, wrapped the fish and chips in newspaper, took your money and that was that. He seemed strange to me. Mother didn't like the fish and chips man because his fingernails were always dirty, and she said anyone who couldn't keep his fingernails clean probably needed a bath! I thought the fish and chips were good and so did Mother, so we kept buying from him despite his dirty fingernails!

We met our landlord, Mr. Styles, only once, and he seemed rude. He was a large, evil-looking man. He was about 6 feet tall and 200 to 250 pounds. He always seemed grumpy.

We met him the day after we moved in; Mr. Styles brought some papers for Father to sign. Since Father wasn't there, Mother said she would sign them. She usually took care of all our financial matters anyway, because Father was away often and not really good with money matters. Anyway, Mr. Styles always seemed in a hurry and was really put out when Mother said she would sign the papers, especially when she had to read every page before she signed it.

"Why do you want to do that, mum?" questioned Mr. Styles.

"I just want to make sure everything is correct before I sign it," explained Mother.

"It's all right, just the way your husband and I agreed!" said Mr. Styles with a slight abruptness in his voice. "Besides, I think it's irregular doing it this way. I made the agreement with your husband, and I think he should sign it."

"Well, he could if he were here, but since he isn't here, I think I'll sign it for the both of us," Mother said. "If you want him to sign it, then you'll just have to wait until he comes home, and I don't know when that will be."

"Well, I don't know, mum, I think…," Mr. Styles trailed off.

"Oh, don't worry about it, Mr. Styles, you got your first month's rent in advance," Mother said firmly.

"I don't like it; no, I don't. Not at all," Mr. Styles said.

He grumbled some more and finally left saying something under his breath about how this ought to be his house anyway.

"What did he mean by that, Mother?" I asked.

"I don't know dear, don't worry about it. I'll tell your Father everything he said when he comes home," Mother replied.

CHAPTER 3

A Christmas to Remember

I loved Mother. She had a way of making every holiday special, even if Father wasn't there, which was most of the time. Sometimes he would be gone for weeks and come home and not tell us anything. He said it was Air Force business, and he couldn't say. The secrecy made me curious and made me wonder if he could be a spy or something. But we lived with it.

It wasn't unusual to celebrate Christmas without Father, but Mother always managed to make it a happy occasion.

Mother would make Christmas cookies and let Nancy and me help. My job was to cut the cookies with the cookie cutters shaped like Christmas trees, Santa Claus, stars and bells.

Mother always rolled out the dough because she said that was the most important part, and it had to be done just right. Nancy helped put the cookies in the oven, and when they were done and cooled down, we both helped ice them. We used red and green frosting most of the time, but sometimes we experimented and used blue or yellow and even white. Then we put candy pieces on them. Some cookies we left plain because Mother said they were the best to dip in coffee or tea. She was right.

During that first winter in England, Father came home a few days before Christmas with all sorts of packages for us. He had a basket full of fruit, candy, meat and cheese. Mother asked where he had gotten all this stuff and how he could afford it. Father gave her his standard answer: Someone gave him the basket as a present and the other stuff he had picked up here and there. Someone at the base was always being transferred back to the states or to Germany, and Father said they would leave all sorts of things behind because they couldn't take it with them.

Now that Father was home I waited for the right time, after he had relaxed a bit, and then asked him if we could explore the tunnels.

"What tunnels?" he exclaimed.

My plan was working so far. I knew if I piqued his curiosity he wouldn't be able to resist going into the tunnels.

"Why the tunnels under the house," I said.

"What tunnels under the house?" he asked.

Just then Mother entered the room.

"William, are you trying to get your Father to go down into those

"But Mother…," I trailed off, trying to say something else but getting no further.

"Listen honey, you know there are spiders down there and how dark and musty it was," she said.

"You mean you've been down there?" Father exclaimed.

"Well, Mr. Walsh showed us what was in the basement and some door leading to some so-called tunnels, but I wouldn't let us go any farther," Mother replied.

"But Mother, remember you said we could explore the tunnels when Father came home, remember?" I pleaded politely.

"What tunnels? Will someone please tell me what tunnels you're talking about?" Father asked in frustration.

"Well, dear, Mr. Walsh says there is a tunnel under the house, but it's really cold down there and creepy!" Mother said.

"Mr. Walsh says there are lots of tunnels and one goes all the way into the next town, Ely, I think, and Mr. Thatcher says he's been in the tunnels, and he says there are skeletons and," I interjected excitedly.

"Hold on there, William, hold on. What's this about skeletons, and who's Mr. Thatcher?" Father asked.

"Mr. Thatcher is the butcher," Mother explained.

"What would the butcher know about tunnels under this house?" Father questioned.

"Well, dear, we were over there the other day buying some pork chops, and Mr. Thatcher said some of the townspeople had toured the tunnels at the invitation of Rev. Holder," Mother replied.

"Who's Rev. Holder?" he queried.

"Why, he's the vicar of the church, and we found out, by the way, that he really owns this house," she said.

"What?" Father asked.

"That's right dear," Mother said. "When Mr. Styles came over with the lease papers for me to sign he told me that Rev. Holder owns this property. I guess Mr. Styles is just the landlord. He didn't seem too happy about it either, and he was rude!"

"Rude, how?" Father asked, frowning.

"Well, he kept going on about you making the deal with him and how it was your responsibility to sign the papers, and, well, he was just very rude, that's all," she said.

"He was, was he? Well, we'll see about that. The next time I see him I'll suggest to him that he might be more careful how he speaks to you!" Father said.

"Now, Henry, don't go and get upset. It really isn't worth it. You know how your temper is," Mother replied.

"Can we go down and see the skeletons?" I asked, hoping to get my parents back on topic.

"Now, see what you've done, Henry, you've got him all excited about going down there in those tunnels!" Mother said.

"I've got him excited!" Father exclaimed. "It sounds like he got excited all by himself, and so what if there are tunnels under the house? What's wrong with exploring them?"

"Yeah, can we go now Father? Can we go now?" I pleaded.

"I don't see why not. You got your flashlight?" Father asked.

"Yes, Father, I do," I replied.

Just then Nancy entered the room. "What's going on?" she asked.

"Father is going to take us down to explore the tunnels," I said.

"Really?" Nancy asked.

"Now, Nancy, I don't think you need to go down there. I don't think any of us need to go down there," Mother said.

"Now, Mary, what can it hurt? I'm sure there isn't much to see, and if there is, well, it could be fun," Father said.

"Yeah. Come on, Mother, we'll protect you," I said.

"Protect me; I'm not afraid." she said firmly.

"Well, that settles it then," Father said. "Come on, let's go."

"We need to get the key from Mr. Walsh," Mother said.

"No, we don't. I know where he puts them," I said.

"You do? And how do you know that?" Mother asked.

"I saw him put them on a nail behind the kitchen door," I replied.

"Our kitchen door?" Mother asked.

"No, the old kitchen, the one downstairs," I said.

"I think we need to get permission from Mr. Walsh before we go trespassing down there," Mother declared.

"We're not trespassing. We live here!" Father yelled.

"Oh, all right, but let me get a jacket first, and you two children get jackets too, understand?" Mother said.

"Yes, Mother," was our dutiful reply.

With our jackets on and flashlights in hand we proceeded downstairs to the old kitchen. The key ring was right where I said they would be. Father unlocked the door and we went down into the basement. The door to the tunnels was locked, but that key was on the ring as well. The door creaked loudly when we opened it; that same rush of stale, musty air hit our nostrils.

It was dark – very dark. The floor was full of dirt and dust, and it blew up into the air as we walked. Father said to walk slowly and try not to stir up the dust too much. The tunnel seemed to be empty as far as we could tell. I knew the spiders must be there, lurking in the darkness. I stayed close to Father.

The tunnel abruptly split into two passageways. One went right and the other left. We decided to go left. We went about 10 or 15 feet into it when it opened into a large room. We could see large wooden racks around the edge of the room. The room wasn't very large, maybe 25 feet long and about the same in width. At the end of the room there was an archway into another room.

As we entered the room Mother screamed, "What's that, Henry?"

We looked over toward the wall, and there it was. A skeleton was hanging by chains against the wall.

"It's a skeleton all right," Father said. "Some guy probably didn't pay his rent!"

"That's not funny," Mother huffed.

Nancy and I laughed anyway, but it was creepy. We saw other chains hanging from the wall, but these did not hold skeletons. This room was bigger than the first one, maybe twice the size. It did not go anywhere; it was a dead end.

"Let's get out of here," Mother said solemnly.

"Oh, come on, Mary, we just got here, and we haven't seen where the other tunnel goes," Father cajoled.

"The other must be the one that leads to the other town," I said.

"Let's go back and see what it looks like," Father said.

So we retraced our steps back to the split. This time we went right. This tunnel seemed very long. We went quite a way before we entered another room. This one was large and empty as far as we could tell. There was a door at the far end.

"That must be the door to the tunnel that goes to that other city," I said excitedly.

Father tried the door, but it was locked. The keys on the ring would not open it – or it was stuck. Anyway, Father could not budge it.

"Can we go now?" Mother asked. "There is nothing here but dust and bad air."

"I guess you're right," Father replied.

So we started back. All of a sudden Father tripped over something on the floor. It was in the corner near the door that wouldn't open. Our flashlights revealed a large shape.

Father bravely reached down and picked it up.

"It's a sort of package or something," he said, surprised.

It was covered in dust and seemed to be wrapped in a type of leather binder.

"We'll just take it with us and see what it is when we get back upstairs," Father said.

Once again we retraced our steps. We were careful to lock the door and put the keys back where we found them before returning to our apartment.

Father placed the package on the kitchen table.

"I think we better wipe it off with a cloth first, don't you think?" Mother asked.

Mother got a cloth, wet it a little and began to wipe off the layers of dirt that covered the package. It was leather all right, and very old looking. The leather was stiff and cracked, but the wet cloth loosened it a bit. Mother unwrapped the leather to reveal some sort of cloth beneath it. It was thick and oily. She got the leather wrapping off with some help from Father and unwrapped the oilcloth.

Whatever was under there was large and heavy. Mother took off one layer after another, all oily. Father said he thought it was some sort of book. Layer after layer came off until we got to some paperlike oil wrapper. We took the paper off and beheld a large book with writing on it. It looked very old.

Carefully, Mother opened the cover and there it was.

"Oh, my heavens, Henry! It's a Bible!" exclaimed Mother excitedly.

"Are you sure?" he asked.

"I've seen pictures of very old Bibles," Mother said, "and this one looks like … oh, no, it couldn't be!"

"Couldn't be what?" Father asked.

"A Gutenberg Bible!" Mother said reverently.

"What's a Gutenberg Bible?" I asked.

"It's the first book ever printed," she replied.

"The first book ever printed!" Nancy exclaimed.

"That's right," Mother answered. "Johann Gutenberg invented the printing press around 1455, and the first book he printed was the Bible. This could be one of those."

"Oh, that's impossible," Father said.

"Well, we must have this checked out, because if it is a Gutenberg Bible it's worth a fortune and belongs in a museum," Mother answered.

"But we found it and it's ours," Father declared.

"It's not ours, Henry. We found it in on this property and therefore it belongs to Rev. Holder, or the town, or something, but we can't keep it," Mother said.

"Why not?" he asked.

"That's right, finders keepers," I interjected.

"Do you know what this book is worth?" Father asked.

"No and neither do you," Mother replied. "It has to be given to the proper authorities."

"But Mary, if this really is a Gutenberg Bible it's priceless. We could retire and have everything we've always wanted," Father implored.

"But it's not the right thing to do," Mother said firmly.

"No one would know," Nancy said.

"You two children stay out of this. This is something your Father and I have to decide for ourselves," Mother admonished.

After many hours of arguing, Mother won and Father agreed to take the Bible next door to Rev. Holder. The next day we all went to the church looking for Rev. Holder. On the way to the church we walked through the graveyard.

I'd never seen grave markers so old. There were some with dates that were recent: 1912, 1842, 1835. Then there were others with dates so old that we could barely read them. We saw one from 1416 and another from 1291. That is old!

Some had names we could read; others we couldn't. The graveyard seemed well cared for, but there were still weeds growing up between the markers. It was one of those graveyards like you see in the movies, all gray and creepy looking. The path to the church led right through it.

When we got to our destination we didn't know whether to go to the church or to the little house beside it. We assumed that the vicar lived in the little house.

We decided to go to the church first. The large front doors were made of solid oak. They were bigger than the ones on our house. We went inside, and no one was about. The church was long and narrow with high ceilings. Each stained-glass window depicted a different biblical scene. It was really beautiful. It was cold inside; I didn't know how they could heat some place like this when they had services.

As we admired the church Rev. Holder seemed to appear from nowhere with another man we didn't know. The Rev. Holder was tall, maybe 6 feet, and slender. He looked like he was about 40, but had a baby face, light brown hair and a soft voice.

"Good morning," he said cheerily. "How may I help you?"

"Good morning," Father said. "We're here to see you about a very important matter."

"And what might that be?" questioned Rev. Holder.

"Well, we were exploring down in the tunnels beneath the home next door …."

"Oh, you must be the American family that just moved in. I've been meaning to come by and welcome you. I'm the Rev. Holder, vicar of this church, and this is my assistant Mr. Cox," he said.

Rev. Holder extended his hand and Father took it.

"I'm Henry and this is my wife Mary," Father said. "These are my two children, Nancy and William."

"I'm very pleased to meet you," Rev. Holder said. "Now what can I do for you?"

"Well, as I started to say, we were exploring down in the tunnels, and we found something that might be of interest to you." Father answered.

"And what might that be?" the reverend asked.

"Well, we think it's a Gutenberg Bible, but we're not sure," Father said.

"A Gutenberg Bible! You're kidding!" Rev. Holder exclaimed.

"No, we're not kidding. Here, Mary, give me the package. Is there some place where we can go so we can show this to you?" Father inquired.

"Yes, come right into my study. Right this way. Mr. Cox here is a bit of a history buff so he might help identify this book you have," Rev. Holder said as he led us down the aisle of the church toward the back.

We went down a short hallway and through a door and into his office. It looked more like a living room than an office. There was a nice fire going in the stone fireplace. Above the fireplace was a mantle with two pictures on it; one I guessed to be Rev. Holder's mother and the other was him standing next to a man Mother later said was Winston Churchill. In the middle of the mantle was a trophy that read "First Place Distance Run, Cambridge, 1934."

There was a couch with red cushions and two high-backed chairs, also in red. All seemed very old. There was an old desk with a beautiful lamp on it with a multicolored glass top. The room was lined with bookshelves, indicating that Rev. Holder was a bookworm. There was a coffee table in front of the couch. Over to the side of the room was a steaming silver teapot on a potbellied stove. The English have tea all the time, so I was not surprised that water was boiling.

"Well, let's see what we have here," Rev. Holder said.

"We kept it wrapped in the oil cloth we found it in because we didn't want to damage it, especially if it was valuable," Mother explained.

Mother laid the Bible on the table and began to unwrap it. I watched Rev. Holder's eyes as she unwrapped the Bible. They seemed to get bigger and bigger. When she finally got it open, the Rev. Holder gasped, "Oh, my heavens!"

"What? Do you think it's valuable?" Father asked.

"Valuable! Oh yes, it's valuable all right. It is a Gutenberg Bible as far as I can tell. What do you think Mr. Cox?" the reverend asked his associate.

"I've seen one in the Museum of Natural History in London. This looks genuine to me. My word, could it really be a Gutenberg Bible?" Mr. Cox wondered.

"We felt the right thing to do was bring it to you since you own the house where we found it, and I guess it really sort of belongs to the town," Mother offered.

"You were right, mum, it belongs to the whole town. Wait till everyone hears of this; you'll be celebrities for sure!" the reverend said.

"Really?" I exclaimed.

"Oh, yes, a find like this doesn't come along very often. I've got to think of what to do," Rev. Holder said thoughtfully.

"What do you mean?" Father asked.

"Well, we've got to send this to London to authenticate it first, and then I guess it will go into the museum. I'll call the museum and tell them what you've found and see what they want to do, but I'm sure they will want to see it right away. Meanwhile the whole town needs to hear of this great discovery. You'll be celebrities, all of you," he said again.

"All of us?" I asked.

"Sure you will," Rev. Holder replied. "All of you were present when your Father found it, so sure, you'll all be famous, probably get your picture in the *Times* and everything."

"You think we'll get on TV?" Nancy asked.

"Well, who knows? With a discovery this big, maybe so, maybe so," Rev. Holder replied.

"Now, Nancy, what on earth do you want to go on TV for?" Mother asked.

"But, Mother, it's so exciting. Why shouldn't we be on TV? Father found it didn't he? And we were there when he did, so why not get on TV?" Nancy replied.

"Let's not get carried away children. There is no need to build this thing all out of proportion," Father cautioned. "Well, Reverend, we'll leave the Bible with you now. Good luck. Come on, everyone. Let's go home."

"Thank you all so much. I'll call London right away, and I'll let you know what happens. Mr. Cox, I hope you won't be upset, but would it be too much of an imposition to ask you to stay here and watch this Bible?" Rev. Holder asked.

"Not at all reverend. You know I have no family. I'll be glad to stay here as long as necessary," Mr. Cox said.

"That's fine. Well, Merry Christmas," Rev. Holder called out as we left.

So that was that. We had taken what was probably the most valuable book in the world and given it to Rev. Holder, vicar of a church in Soham, England. He would call the museum in London, tell the directors about the Bible and they would want it for their museum. And what would we get? A little publicity in the paper, maybe. Even though I was young, I could tell Father was not happy about this. I knew Mother was right and we had to give the Bible back to the town, but it was hard to do, especially when you knew that the book was worth a lot of money. Who knows? Maybe they'd give us a reward or something. That's it, a reward! Why, it could be thousands of dollars, or pounds, or whatever, but surely there would be a reward of some kind!

We found the Bible on Friday, took it to Rev. Holder on Saturday and on Sunday he announced the great find to his congregation. Before we could have our morning breakfast we began to hear the news that was spreading all over town – faster than a hare running from a fox.

First, Mr. and Mrs. Walsh knocked on our door and congratulated us on the find, but I could tell they were jealous, especially since Mr. Walsh had been in those tunnels so many times before and never found it. They were trying to be sincere, but even I could tell they were jealous. Mother noticed it too and commented about it to Father. They didn't think I heard them, but I could hear them even though they were trying to be quiet. It's a kid thing.

Next, Mr. Styles showed up asking a million questions about the Bible: Where we found it, when, and so forth. Father was polite, but I could tell he was steaming underneath. None of us really liked Mr.

Styles. He was mean looking and seemed agitated when he spoke, like he was about to jump at you or something. We knew he really wanted the house because he told us how he had offered Rev. Holder a lot of money for it, but Rev. Holder would not sell. Now that we had found the Bible I guess Mr. Styles thought the Bible would have been his if the house were in his possession. Again, we could tell he was not happy about the whole thing even though he pretended to be happy for us.

By Monday everyone in town knew and Tuesday was Christmas, so we went into town to get some things for our holiday dinner. As we walked down the street people stopped and talked to us or waved to us or just smiled. It really was like we were celebrities!

At the bakery Mr. and Mrs. Moore started congratulating us before we got in the door. What a rare find they said, and how wonderful it was for the town. The British Broadcasting Corp., a k a BBC, would surely want to come to Soham and interview us they said. Maybe someone from the *London Times* or some other newspaper would interview us. Oh, it was so exciting they said, just like a movie or something. Just think, they said, they had been in those tunnels themselves and probably walked right past that Bible without seeing it. Wasn't it wonderful that we had found it?

We got our bread and left feeling guilty, like we had stolen something from them. That's the way the rest of our shopping trip was that day. Everywhere we went we seemed to feel guilty that we had found the Bible and not someone else. It seemed that almost everyone had been in the tunnels at one time or another and wondered why they had not discovered the Bible.

Mr. Thatcher, the butcher, said if he had found it he would have sold it to the highest bidder and then left Soham forever. There was no question that Mr. Thatcher had no love for Soham, but we didn't know why.

Mrs. Wallis, over at the post office, was excited for us too, but she also let us know that if she had found it she could have afforded to move to Florida with her sister. I think Miss Stone at the candy store puzzled me the most. She didn't seem happy at all that we found the Bible and really seemed agitated that we had given it to Rev. Holder. It was like she resented it or something. Maybe I was judging her wrong, but I could usually tell how someone felt about things. I guess I got that from Mother. She could tell what anybody was thinking and was usually right, too. I know Miss Stone didn't like what happened because she didn't offer me any free candy like she had done every other time we had been in her store.

Rev. Holder came by later that day to report on his call to the museum. They were very excited about the find and wanted to get the Bible as soon as possible. He said he had made arrangements for them to pick it up on Wednesday. I guess they didn't want to waste any time, but that seemed like a rush to me. That would be the day after Christmas. Given the great value of the Bible, I suppose the museum wanted to put it in safe keeping as soon as possible. Well, that made sense to me. If I had something as valuable as this Bible was supposed to be, I would want to keep it safe, too. On the other hand, Rev. Holder had Mr. Cox watching it, so I was sure it would be safe.

My mind was on other things, namely Christmas. I wondered what I would get. I was hoping for more knights and maybe a football. I had searched around the house for presents but was unable to find Mother's and Father's hiding places. I'm glad I didn't find anything because last year I found all my presents and was disappointed on Christmas Day.

I had a really nice present for Mother. I hoped she would like it. I had found it in the BX, which was the base exchange or store. It was a vase from France. It was about 7 or 8 inches tall with gold handles on the sides. It was a sort of green color with pretty roses painted on it. It had cost me $8, so I hoped she liked it. I got Father some men's cologne, and I loved the smell of it. You could smell it throughout the house. For Nancy, I got a bottle of perfume. The lady told me it was from France and all the good perfume came from France, or so I had heard.

Our tree was huge. Father had come home with it tied to the top of our car, which he used for getting to and from base. The high ceiling of our large living was perfect for the tree – it fit beautifully. It must have been taller than 10 feet high because we ran out of decorations; Mother decided we would make some more. We had lots of candy wrappers from the candy we had bought at Miss Stone's candy store; we folded them into a chain. That was great fun because we had to eat more candy to make the chain longer. But the chain was no match for the tree – it seemed to disappear once we draped it on the branches.

That was no problem, Father said, because we could pop some popcorn and string it together like he used to do when he was a kid. So we popped popcorn and strung it together until we ran out of it. Now the tree began to look like something. Next we took pipe cleaners and made them into people. We used small nuts for their heads and crate paper for the clothes. We painted faces on them, and they began to look pretty good. After we had made about 20 of these, we put them on the tree. Finally, we had enough decorations to do the tree justice. We also put some small candles on the tree and lit them. It was really beautiful seeing the tree all lit up. The flicker of the candlelight on the ornaments made for a special display of colors that bounced off the walls in a concert of lights.

We had cookies and milk for a snack, and then Nancy and I were allowed to open up one present each before going to bed. That was our family tradition: open one present, go to bed and then Santa came in the middle of the night. My parents put just a few presents under the tree before we went to bed; they put the rest out after we were asleep. That way we were excited to see all the presents when we got up.

Nancy and I rarely slept while we waited for Santa to come, but we had to go through the ritual anyway. Father would make some noise outside or ring some sleigh bells or something. Then he would yell "Ho, ho, ho and Merry Christmas."

A few minutes later Mother would come and tell us that Santa had been there and we could get up. I don't know what time that was, but it was usually late, at least late for us. We would get up and open all the rest of our presents; the really hard part was going back to bed. Here I had gotten all these neat toys and then couldn't play with them until morning. What a gyp!

I really got a kick out of my family opening the gifts I got them. To me this was more exciting than opening up my own gifts. Mother always told me that it was more blessed to give than receive. I guess she was right because that's how I felt.

The next morning was Christmas Day, and it was beautiful. The sun was up and shining on the snow. I looked out my window and saw little bird tracks in the snow on my windowsill. I had put some cookies out on the sill the night before for them to eat. They were all gone, so I suppose the birds got them.

I couldn't wait to get to play with my toys. Along with knights and a big red fire engine with a long ladder, I also got a genuine National Football League football. I wouldn't be able to play with it right away because of the snow, but as soon as the snow melted I was planning to get out in the yard and kick it as far as I could. I also got a sweater from my grandmother in Virginia. It was too big for me, but it really felt warm that day because it was bitter cold. I also got a new jacket – a real Air Force flight jacket from Father. It had zippers in the sleeve and everything. It was super cool, and I wore it the first chance I got. Nancy gave me a large bag of marbles for my collection. I was very proud of my marble collection. I was good at shooting marbles and had won most of the marbles I had.

But those presents paled in comparison to my parents' biggest surprise: a Corgi puppy. I couldn't believe it. We named her Goldie because her hair was like gold, with a shine on it. How Mother and Father kept this puppy a secret amazed me.

Mother said they got her from Miss Stone. She had Corgis and one of them had a litter of puppies. Miss Stone agreed to keep the puppy until Father picked her up on Christmas Eve. Goldie really wasn't my present – she was for the whole family – but I liked to think she was for me. She bounced all over the place and looked like a little fur ball when she rolled over.

The first thing she did was tinkle on the rug, but that was to be expected from a puppy who was only 12 weeks old. Goldie was the runt of the litter and the one Mother picked out for us. She would bring many happy days to us or so I had hoped.

CHAPTER 4

Tragedy in the Church Office

Christmas had been perfect so far; I didn't think anything could spoil it. We had a wonderful breakfast of English pork sausages, the kind that split open in the pan when they're cooking, thick slices of toasted bread spread with strawberry jam, eggs over easy and nice cups of hot chocolate with little marshmallows oozing over the top of the mugs. I thought I would burst from eating so much.

After breakfast Father went into the living room to read the newspaper while Mother and Nancy cleaned the kitchen. My job was to take a nice plate of Mother's cookies over to Rev. Holder. Here was the chance to wear my new flight jacket for the first time.

Mother put several types of cookies on the plate, mostly those that were decorated the nicest. I put on my jacket and went off with the plate of cookies. Boy, was it ever cold outside! The sun was up because it was almost 9 in the morning, but it still was freezing. I think all the birds were frozen too, because I didn't hear a peep out of any of them, even the crows. That seemed odd because the crows were always noisy, cold or no cold.

The snow was deeper than I expected. It must have really snowed heavily last night. The path to the church led through a gate on our property, through the graveyard and straight to the back door of the church. It was unlocked so I went in. I think the inside of the church was colder than it was outside. I could see my breath inside the church.

Rev. Holder's office was in the back, so I decided to look there for him first. I guess I should have gone to his home first, it being Christmas Day, but for some reason I decided to go to his church office first. As I walked down the aisle of the church I thought I heard muffled voices coming from the office. Suddenly, the voices got louder and I heard someone cry out as if they were in pain. I heard a loud thump like something had fallen on the floor. Then it was quiet.

I got scared so I ducked into one of the confessional booths and hid. It seemed like an eternity before I heard anything else, but eventually

I heard someone coming. I couldn't see out of the curtain without moving it and giving away my hiding place, but there was a slight rip in the material. Someone went past quickly and they were carrying something in their arms, but I couldn't tell what it was. The odor of fish, or something that smelled like fish, wafted through the curtain. Whoever it was went out the back door.

I felt it was safe to come out, so I left the confessional booth and headed for Rev. Holder's office. The door was slightly open, but I knocked anyway to be polite. There was no answer so I tried to open it, but I couldn't. Something on the floor was blocking it. I pushed harder and gradually moved whatever was blocking the door.

I peeked my head in the door and saw what was obstructing the door: Mr. Cox. He had fallen or something because there was a pool of blood on the floor by his head. I squeezed into the room and knelt down beside him. I tried to wake him, but he wasn't breathing. Now I was really scared.

I ran home just as fast as I could, slipping down twice in the snow. I ran in the front door yelling at the top of my lungs.

"Mother, Father, come quick! It's Mr. Cox. He's hurt, come quick!"

Father came first. "What is it, William? Calm down, tell me what happened," he said.

"I was taking the cookies Mother fixed for Rev. Holder, but when I got into the church it sounded like voices coming from his office. They were yelling, so I hid in the confessional booth," I said.

"You did what?" Father asked.

"I hid in the confessional booth. Then someone came out and ran past me. I waited for a time and then went to Rev. Holders' office. I found Mr. Cox laying on the floor and there is a lot of blood. He's not breathing; I think he may be dead," I said, out breath.

"Who is dead? What are you talking about, William?" Mother asked.

"Mr. Cox, Rev. Holder's assistant. I think he's dead. Come quick!" I said with urgency.

Finally convinced that I wasn't fooling, my family rushed with me to the church. We found the body just where I said it was laying in a pool of blood. It was horrible. Nancy almost passed out. Mother, who was very excitable during emergencies, seemed very calm.

Both Father and Mother examined Mr. Cox and decided he was dead. Father used the phone in Rev. Holder's office and called the police. The constable – that's what they call policemen in England – came quickly. He called an ambulance, which arrived and took Mr. Cox away.

Mother tried to take Nancy and me into the church where we wouldn't see all of this, but we could still hear what they were saying. Father told the constable that I discovered the body and that someone had run out just prior to that. Both he and the constable agreed that this must have been a murder.

Just think of it! A murder right here next door to our house, and I heard it and maybe saw the criminal, or I thought I did. I smelled whoever it was anyway. The perpetrator smelled of fish. I figured it out already; it was the fish guy behind the post office. He must be the murderer. But why would he want to kill Mr. Cox?

The constable told Father that this was too big of a crime for a little town like Soham, so he was going to call Scotland Yard.

"What's Scotland Yard?" I asked Father later.

"Well, William, it's like the English version of the FBI," he said.

"You mean they're going to send FBI guys here to Soham?" I asked.

"No, Scotland Yard men," He said.

Just then Mother entered the room. "I'm so sorry that William had to witness so horrible a thing," she said.

"It wasn't so horrible," I said "I didn't really see anything except some blood."

"That's what I mean. Oh, Henry, it's so awful. My little boy seeing such a thing," she said.

"Now, calm down, dear. It'll be all right. William doesn't seem to be upset, so why should you be?" Father asked.

"It's all right, Mother," I said. "I'm OK."

"You may be, but your sister had to have some warm milk and go lay down. She's very upset. Poor dear!" Mother said.

"Why would anyone want to kill Mr. Cox?" I asked.

"I don't know, William," Father answered.

"I know why," Mother said.

"You do?" Father exclaimed.

"Of course, it's very simple. Did anyone see the Bible? When we were in Rev. Holder's office he had it on his coffee table. Was it there today? I don't remember seeing it," she said.

"That's right!" Father said excitedly. "I don't remember seeing it either! Someone must have killed Mr. Cox for the Bible."

"Well, I think we've had enough excitement for one day, and it's time this family settled down and had a rest," Mother announced.

"You're not going to make me take a nap are you?" I asked suspiciously.

"It wouldn't hurt, William. You've had a terrible experience and a little rest would do you good," Mother replied.

So I trudged to my room, or closet. During the day I could at least see the spiders on the ceiling. They stayed up there during the day. At night, well, at night I didn't want to think of what they did, but if I needed to see them I could use my flashlight.

All I could see when I entered the room was Mr. Cox laying in a pool of blood. I had put on an act for my parents, but I was really scared. I must have fallen asleep because the next thing I heard was Mother calling us to lunch. We had planned on having some of the fish and chips we kept telling Father about, but he had gone to the fish stand and it was closed.

That made sense – who would want to work on Christmas Day? Or did it? Was it possible it was closed because the fish guy had killed Mr. Cox and was now on the run? He was probably far from town by now with a priceless Gutenberg Bible. He'd most likely head for London where he could sell it, or maybe he'd catch a boat to France and try to sell it in Europe.

I had it all figured out. When that Scotland Yard guy got here I'd solve the crime for him. I'd be a hero. Maybe I'd even get in the newspapers or on TV. Wow! I'd surprise Mother and Father. I wouldn't say anything until the Scotland Yard man arrived.

Lunch was tuna fish sandwiches and potato chips. We were all looking forward to dinner because Mother had a turkey and all the fixings. Thanks to Mother, Christmas dinner was a special occasion every year. We always named the turkey. I don't know when we started doing this, but it was fun. If it was a tom turkey we gave it a boy's name, and if it was a hen we gave it a girl's name. This year it was a large tom turkey that Mother had purchased from Mr. Thatcher. It weighed more than 25 pounds.

Since it was a tom we called it Fred. Fred seemed like a nice name for a turkey. Mother always made the dressing the day before, and I helped. We took bread and tore it into small pieces. Then we mixed it with spices and chopped up celery and onion. Mother took some of the dressing and baked it in the oven, but most of it was stuffed inside the turkey. Some people have cornbread dressing, and I suppose they like it, but there was nothing like Mother's dressing. She opened the oven once in a while to let us see the turkey. No matter where we were in the house we'd come running when she called out, "I'm checking Fred. Everyone come and see."

She always covered the turkey with aluminum foil until it was almost done and then she took it off so that the turkey got nice and brown. The smell filled the house like no other. That combined with aromas of pumpkin pie and the dressing – well, it was just like heaven. We also had mashed potatoes and gravy, cranberry sauce, a vegetable and, of course, olives. We all loved green and black olives. Nancy and I would fight over who got the last black olive. When it came to turkey, I always asked for a leg because to me that was the best part.

We had our Christmas dinner in spite of the circumstances. Mother was determined to not let anything spoil our holiday especially since Father was home. He wasn't always with us for Christmas, so this was special.

After dinner we sat around the fire while Father read a book, Mother knitted, Nancy looked at her records and I played with my knights. I couldn't help but think of what had happened just a few hours ago. It seemed like a dream, but I knew it was real. Rev. Holder came over to try to make us feel better, but I it didn't help. He was upset to think he had let poor Mr. Cox watch the Bible in the first place, and now he was dead. I think Rev. Holder blamed himself.

Father had several days off for Christmas. This gave us a chance to play ball a little. The snow was heavy, so we played ball inside. Mother did not like this, but since Father was home and he insisted on playing ball in the downstairs hallway, she gave in to his demand. We even shot a pellet gun in the house. Father set up a target at the end of the hallway, and we placed the gun on a footstool on top of a pillow. The pillow rest made it easier for me to shoot the gun, which was quite heavy. Father placed a target on a cardboard box and we shot at that. I got pretty good at it. We also played darts. This was an English game, but we loved it. The whole family could play. If you played it properly, it was kind of hard but it was fun. There were many holes in the wall where we missed the target.

We were throwing my baseball when there was a knock at the door.

"I'll get it," I yelled.

I ran to the front door, and when I opened it there stood a tall man in a long gray trench coat and a bowler (a funny looking round hat). He was at least 6 foot 2 and had gray hair that was cut very short. He had a handlebar moustache and wore a gray wool suit with a vest that had a gold pocket watch and chain in the side pocket.

"Good day, lad, I'm Inspector Edwards of Scotland Yard," he said.

"Come on in," I said. "I'll tell Mother and Father that you're here."

So I led Inspector Edwards into our living room and introduced him to my family.

"I understand that your son was the first one to see Mr. Cox after he was killed," Inspector Edwards said.

"That's right," Father answered.

"Might I inquire as to why he was in the church at the time?" Inspector Edwards asked.

"I sent him over with a plate of Christmas cookies for Rev. Holder, but he wasn't there," Mother replied.

"I know why Mr. Cox he was killed," I said.

"Now, just hold on there, William," Father said, "let the inspector ask the questions."

"You know why he was killed?" the inspector asked.

"Well, we think we know why he was killed," Mother said.

"And why do you think he was killed?" the inspector asked again.

"Well, we think someone killed him to get the Bible," Mother explained.

"What Bible?" inquired the inspector.

"Oh, I'm sorry, Inspector, I thought you knew about the Bible," she said.

"What Bible is that you're speaking of, mum?" he asked again.

"You'd better tell him, Henry," Mother said.

"Sure, yes, of course, the Bible," Father said. "We found this old Bible, a Gutenberg Bible to be exact, and we turned it over to Rev. Holder. He called the Museum of Natural History in London and told them what was found. They were supposed to send someone to pick it up, but I guess they'll never get the chance because the Bible is missing."

"How do you know the Bible is missing?" the inspector asked.

"Well, it wasn't there when we were in his office. He told his assistant Mr. Cox to watch it and it was on the coffee table the last time we saw it," Father said.

"Maybe Rev. Holder took it to his house to look at it," Inspector Edwards said.

"I think I know who did it," I volunteered.

"You do, do you? Well, let's hear what you have to say lad," Inspector Edwards said.

"When I took the cookies over I heard voices coming from Rev. Holder's office. The voices were muffled so I couldn't tell what they were saying, but they got louder, like they were yelling at each other," I said. "Anyway, I hid in the confessional booth, and I heard this sound like something falling on the floor. Then there was no sound at all. I waited for a few minutes, and then I saw someone rush past the booth, and it looked like they had something under their arm like a big package or sack."

"Did you see their face, lad?" the inspector asked.

"No, I couldn't tell who it was, but I did smell fish," I said.

"Fish?" he asked.

"Yes, fish," I confirmed. "I think it was that fish and chips guy."

"What fish and chips guy?" the inspector demanded.

"There is a man who sells fish and chips behind the post office, Inspector," I said.

"That's right," Mother agreed.

"I went to his stand yesterday, but it was closed," Father added.

"Do you know his name?" the inspector asked Mother.

"No," she answered.

"Well, I'll check this out later, but I just need to ask William here a few more questions if you don't mind," the inspector said.

"We don't mind at all," Mother said.

"Now, William, you said you hid in the confessional booth?" the inspector asked.

"That's right," I said.

"And you didn't see anyone clearly, just a shadow running by?" he continued.

"That's right," I said.

"Can you tell me what you did when you left the booth?" Inspector Edwards asked.

"Yes, sir. I waited for a few minutes in the booth because I was scared, but after some time passed I went into Rev. Holder's office. The door was blocked by something on the floor, but I squeezed inside. Then I saw Mr. Cox. He was laying on the floor, and there was blood by his head," I told the inspector.

"Do you know what time this was?" he asked.

"Yes, about nine o'clock," I said.

"What did you do then?" the inspector asked.

"I came home and got Mother and Father," I said.

"Did you see this Bible your Father was telling me about?" he asked.

"No, sir, it wasn't there," I replied.

"Would you recognize this Bible if you saw it?" Inspector Edwards asked.

"Oh, yes, sir. I was there when we found it; I know just what it looks like," I said excitedly.

"Just where did you find this Bible?" he asked.

"Father found it in the tunnel," I told him.

"What tunnel?" the inspector queried.

"There are some tunnels under this house," Father told the inspector.

"There are?" Inspector Edwards asked.

"Yes, there are several, even one that is supposed to go to the next town, but we've never been able to open the door to that one. We found the Bible in one of the tunnels, and then we turned it over to Rev. Holder," Father said.

Inspector Edwards looked puzzled and asked, "Why did you give it to him?"

"He owns this house," Mother replied.

"Oh, I see," the inspector said. "I guess that's all I need for now. I'll be calling on you again later if you don't mind. I need to speak to the Rev. Holder and some of the other townspeople first, so I'll be off. It was nice meeting all of you. I can find my own way out. If you need me I'll be staying at the Boar's Head Inn in town."

So that was the inspector from Scotland Yard. He was nice. I was betting he would look for that fish and chips guy first; I know I would. Who else would smell like fish? If I were the fish and chips guy, I'd be hundreds of miles from here by now.

The rest of the day it snowed heavily and all the next day. We went into town to get some bread and all we heard about was the terrible murder of Mr. Cox. The whole town seemed to be in an uproar. I was a celebrity because I found the body. Everyone seemed to know all the details. I guess they had all talked to Inspector Edwards, but why would he tell everyone about me finding the body?

Father said he'd never do that, at least if he was a good inspector. Maybe the local constable told some people. There seemed to be no other explanation. Everywhere we went people stopped us and said it must have been a terrible thing for me to discover the dead body. We also found out that Inspector Edwards had told everyone not to leave town until he was finished with his investigation, but that was not to be very long because the next thing we found out was startling to say the least.

Mrs. Moore told us that the inspector had made an arrest already. She said he had arrested Ted Wellington, the fish and chips guy. So that was his name! Mrs. Moore went on to tell us that Mr. Wellington had a police record. She knew because the local constable was her cousin, and he told her. The police had done a background check on Mr. Wellington and found out he had been in prison for burglary or something like that. Anyway, he was an ex-con. She said that was enough for the inspector to arrest him until further evidence could be found. Evidently Mr. Cox had been hit on the head by a blunt instrument, according to the coroner's report, but the murder weapon was missing. The coroner also said he was killed between 8 and 8:30 a.m. Everyone also seemed to know that the Bible was missing. Mrs. Moore said that Mr. Wellington didn't have it, or at least he said he didn't, so the Bible was still missing. At least there was someone in jail, probably the murderer. The Bible would probably show up in Mr. Wellington's apartment.

The case seemed to have been solved. This Inspector Edwards was good all right; he had solved the case quickly, with my help, of course. I wondered if there would be a reward for Mr. Wellington's capture, or maybe for the Bible, when it was found. All in all, it had been a busy day for my family. We were all tired and went to bed early.

The next day Inspector Edwards stopped by to thank us for our help. He said he was returning to London with Mr. Wellington. Mr. Wellington could not give a satisfactory alibi for his whereabouts on the morning of the murder. That and the fact that I had smelled fish when the suspect had passed by the confessional, and his previous record, was enough for the inspector to have a pretty clear-cut case. He said he had arrested Mr. Wellington for murder and was taking him to London until he could stand trial.

He also told us that I would have to testify in the trial, but that would most likely not be until sometime in the spring because of the backlog of cases at Scotland Yard. He thanked us again, left his card and was off to London. He didn't say anything about the missing Bible, and we didn't ask. Maybe he had found it. I guess we'd find out about it later. The whole town was still gossiping about the murder, so I figured someone would know about the Bible. I was sure Mrs. Moore or someone would tell us.

Christmas vacation was over and my family returned to normal routines. Father went back to his base; Nancy and I went back to school. My life went back to normal – for three short weeks.

I came home from school one day to find out that Mr. Wellington was back in town selling fish and chips.

"How could that be?" I asked Mother.

"Well, William, it seems that there was not enough evidence to hold Mr. Wellington. According to the paper, Inspector Edwards could not find the weapon that killed Mr. Cox or any fingerprints at the scene. A search of Mr. Wellington's apartment turned up no clues and no Bible. It's still missing. With no evidence the judge had no choice. So he let Mr. Wellington go. The paper also said that the investigation was continuing and that Inspector Edwards was headed back to Soham to interview everyone in town," Mother explained.

"But Mother, they might have let the murderer go free," I said.

"We don't know that he is the murderer, William, and besides, Scotland Yard knows what they are doing or they wouldn't have let him go," she said.

"I guess so, but it sounds funny to me," I said.

Or did it? I asked myself. That made me think of the funeral, yes, the funeral for Mr. Cox. Why didn't I think of that before? The fish smell. I told myself to tell Inspector Edwards when he came back to town.

I didn't have to wait long because Inspector Edwards came back to Soham the next day. We heard he was in town from Mrs. Moore. He was staying at the same inn he'd stayed at before and was planning to interview several people. I wondered when he'd get to me.

Mr. Wellington went back to selling fish, but I don't think he sold much because everyone thought he had killed Mr. Cox. Gossip was running rampant through town, but Mother tried to protect Nancy and me from it. She said she had enough of this murder and didn't want to hear any more about it. I, on the other hand, was curious and tried to figure it out.

Finally, Inspector Edwards came back to our house, and I got to talk to him again. I told him that the day of the funeral for Mr. Cox I was standing in a crowd of people when, suddenly, I smelled the fish smell that I had smelled the day of the murder. I looked around, but couldn't figure out where the odor was coming from. There were too many people milling about and being shorter than the adults I couldn't see over anyone. I tried to go through the crowd and see if I could smell it again but I couldn't.

The inspector thanked me for the information, asked a few more questions and then left. He said he'd be back if necessary.

I had thought it funny that I smelled that same smell when Mr. Wellington was in jail in London. How could that be?

Now I was confused. Somehow the Gutenberg Bible was involved in this murder, and I was going to try and find out how. However, I had to do it without Mother knowing or she'd be mad at me. I knew Mother would not let me run around town alone, so I decided I would do some detective work on my own after school. All I had to do was get off the bus and head for town instead of home. The bus left me at the end of our driveway and it was so long and curved Mother couldn't see me get off. Once I was off the bus I could head for one of the stores and catch up on the local gossip. I could get to at least one store before I'd have to run home.

Mother wouldn't suspect anything. I didn't think of it as lying, but as helping Inspector Edwards solve a murder case. The bus took so long to get from my school to home that it was always late anyway; Mother would never know.

CHAPTER 5

Inspector Will

The first day I tried my little investigative adventure I went to the bakery because Mrs. Moore was related to the local constable, who seemed to have a loose tongue. Mrs. Moore was glad to see me, but wondered where Mother was. I told her that I just got off the bus and really wanted to buy one of her delicious pastries. She gave me an apple pastry and said it was on the house, so I thanked her and then asked her a few questions.

She told me that Inspector Edwards had already interviewed her and her husband.

"There wasn't much to tell him," she said. "We just told him that we were at home together the day of the murder. He asked if we had seen the Bible that was missing and we told him no, but that we had heard about it. We also told him that we had been in those same tunnels and could have discovered that Bible ourselves, but it was just as well we didn't or we may have ended up dead!"

I thanked Mrs. Moore again for the pastry and ran home. Mother never knew the difference.

The next day I did the same thing, and the next until I had visited almost every store in town. I didn't find out much more than I already knew, but I did gather other interesting information.

One very curious bit of information was that Miss Stone, the candy store owner, had been engaged to Rev. Holder before he went into ministry. It seems that Rev. Holder had proposed to her, but the day of the wedding he backed out and didn't even show up for it. According to my source Miss Stone never forgave him for that. He turned to the church and never married. That was interesting. Maybe she wanted to kill him to get back at him, went to the church to do it and found Mr. Cox there instead. But that seemed silly because she was such a nice person, and besides she gave me free candy samples!

During another afternoon investigation I discovered that Mr. Styles would become the owner of the house we lived in if Rev. Holder died. It seems that the house was turned over to the church by the previous owners, who willed it to Rev. Holder with the stipulation that upon his death it would revert to the previous owners or their heirs. The previous owners were Mr. Styles' parents, but they didn't want him to have the responsibility. They liked Rev. Holder (he was their pastor) and believed he would be better at running the house.

My source told me this made Mr. Styles angry because he wanted to sell the house and move away. If the Rev. Holder died the house legally belonged to Mr. Styles. But did that make Mr. Styles a suspect in the death of Mr. Cox? Did he kill Mr. Cox by mistake thinking he was Rev. Holder?

My trips to town after school were an adventure, but I always felt like someone was following me. It was only a feeling I got, but I could swear that someone was behind me on several occasions. When I turned around, no one was there, but it sure felt like there was. I didn't pay attention to my feelings after a while and went about my investigations. I thought if I could find the Bible, or at least find some new information, I could tell Inspector Edwards.

Then one night, while I was laying in bed thinking of spiders falling down on me, I had a thought. What if the murderer hid the Bible in the last place anyone would look for it? What if the murderer had taken it back to the tunnel where it was found? That's it! That's where I would put it if I were going to hide it and not want anyone to know where it was.

The next day was Saturday; I'd go down there and look for myself. I knew where the keys were, and I could do it if I was careful.

Saturday morning came with household chores to do as usual. I had to the feed and water Goldie, dust everywhere and clean my room. Mother went to town to buy some groceries, and Nancy was at some school function. This was the perfect opportunity to slip downstairs and explore the tunnels. I knew the Bible was down there. Where else would the killer hide it? Certainly not where they live or Inspector Edwards would find it.

It had to be there; it was the most logical place. I wondered why Inspector Edwards hadn't thought of it.

I put on my flight jacket, grabbed my trusty Boy Scout flashlight and headed to the kitchen to get the keys. All I needed now was the courage to follow through. That was the hard part. I thought of the spiders that were lurking in the tunnels, just waiting to pounce on me. I thought about my flashlight batteries going dead and leaving me in the dark. I thought about everything that was terrible that could happen to me, and then I remembered something Father had said to me once.

He told me that if I was in a situation where I was really scared that I should close my eyes, take a deep breath and then yell as loud as I could that I was brave and nothing could hurt me. I thought it seemed a bit silly, but if I needed to I would do it. What could it hurt?

I went to the old kitchen to see if Mr. Walsh was there. He wasn't, so I took the keys to the tunnel. I went down the basement stairs and headed for the tunnel door. The keys were heavy, but I managed to get the door open, but the keys stayed stuck in the door!

Well, it didn't matter. I was just going to look inside the tunnels for the Bible; I didn't need the keys for that. My flashlight was working perfectly and I didn't see any spiders, so I went on. I looked first where we found the Bible, but it wasn't anywhere in that room. Then I looked in the second room; no Bible. I was sure it was in the tunnels somewhere, but where? I thought. What if the murderer hid it just inside the door to the long tunnel? No, that couldn't be it because that door wouldn't open; it was stuck. Or was it?

I decided to have a look. I returned to the entry door and wrestled with the keys until I got them out. Then I found the door to the long tunnel and tried the keys. The first key didn't open it, nor did the second, but to my surprise the third key turned in the lock!

I shined the flashlight down on the floor; it looked like this door had recently been opened. A half circle was scraped into the dust on the floor.

I was right. Someone had opened this door and not too long ago either. I pulled with all my strength and the door began to move. The smell was even worse than being in the first tunnels. It smelled like really rotten food. I pulled my jacket up over my nose so the smell wouldn't choke me.

I shined the flashlight down the tunnel; it seemed like there was no end to it. It was long and narrow, with large stones for flooring. I supposed that some of the roof had caved in. I didn't see a Bible nearby, but I figured I would have to go a little farther inside. I took a few steps and then thought I heard something. It sounded like footsteps behind me.

And then that fish smell wafted into my nostrils. I told myself I was imaging the smell.

A loud sound made me jump. I swung the flashlight toward the door and watched it slam shut.

Oh no! It must have been the wind; yes, that's it, the wind. There seemed to be a strong breeze in the tunnel. I'd felt it before. I went back to the door and tried to push it open, but it wouldn't budge. Where were the keys? I'd left them in the door. They were on the other side.

Then I heard the scariest sound of my life – the key turning in the door to lock it.

"Hey!" I shouted. "I'm in here, hey! Let me out, please, hey!"

It was no use. I was locked in. My whole body suddenly felt numb. I couldn't think straight. What was I going to do?

"Please let me out!" I cried.

No one answered. The only thing I could hear was my heart beating faster and faster.

Oh my God, this was not happening to me, I thought. Was this a dream? I wanted to wake up and find Mother standing over me saying it was time for breakfast. But that didn't happen.

This wasn't a dream; this was reality. Now it all began to take shape in my mind. The murderer had followed me into the tunnels and locked me up. He or she must have heard that I saw someone leave the church the day of the murder. Whoever it was must have figured that I might be able to identify them in some way. Maybe the person knew about the fish smell. Whatever the reason, I was trapped. I was shut in this tunnel to die and never be found.

Mother returned from her shopping and called all through the house for me, but there was no answer. She searched everywhere, but her William was not to be seen. She began to get scared.

"William, if you're hiding from me, this is not funny anymore. Come out, please!" she pleaded.

But there was no answer. Now she really began to get upset. With no phone in the house what could she do? She went downstairs to find Mr. or Mrs. Walsh. They had to be about somewhere. She could not find them either.

Now Mother became panicky.

"What can I do now?" Mother asked herself. "I know, William must have followed me downtown to surprise me; maybe he's there. But that can't be it because I would have seen him along the road coming from the house. I'll go downtown and look anyway, but first I'll look outside. He loves to play in the snow. Maybe he's outside. When I get a hold of you William, you're in big trouble."

Mother began her search outside, but found nothing. She went downtown and looked all around, but again found nothing. She stopped in every store and asked everybody, but no one had seen me.

Now she was upset. Mrs. Moore said Inspector Edwards was probably at the Boars Head Inn where he was staying, so she should look there. She headed for the inn, but ran into Inspector Edwards on the way.

"Oh, inspector, am I glad to see you. William is missing," she said.

"William is missing?" the inspector repeated.

"Yes, I've looked everywhere. I've searched the whole house and looked outside. Then I came and searched all over town, but no one has seen him. Oh, Inspector, please, help me," she said, crying.

"Now, now, love, everything will be alright. We'll find William. I'm sure he's just playing somewhere that's all," he said.

"But he would tell me if he had gone from the house. He would have left a note to tell me where he was going, especially if it was important. He always does that. I'm afraid something has happened to him. I can feel it," Mother said.

"Let's go back to your house and search again. I'm sure he'll turn up," the inspector said.

Inspector Edwards and Mother went back to St. Andrew's house and searched everywhere, but I was no where to be found. Mother noticed that my jacket was missing.

"Inspector, look, William's jacket is missing. He wouldn't go out without it because he got it for Christmas and has hardly taken it off," she said.

"Well, if that's true then he must be outside somewhere. You stay here, and I'll search the grounds myself. If he doesn't turn up then I'll get more help. We'll find him, don't you worry, love," the inspector said.

Inspector Edwards searched the grounds around the house, but found nothing. He went back inside and searched again, but found nothing. When he searched the old kitchen he found the door to the basement locked, so he didn't try to get in there. Even if he entered the basement I doubt if he could have heard me if I screamed at the top of my lungs.

As time passed, Inspector Edwards began to get concerned. He also knew what I had been thinking. He knew that others had heard that I had witnessed the killer leaving the scene of the crime, probably with the Bible in tow, and that no one could be sure that I didn't really get a good look at the killer. It was possible the murderer/thief would attempt to get me out of the way. People do strange things when it comes to money.

Unknown to me, Inspector Edwards had the whole town looking for me. He had put out a general alert, complete with a recent picture of me provided by Mother. He had posters made and put them up all over town. The local constable had volunteers looking everywhere. They were just looking in the wrong place.

While the search went on for me, I concentrated on trying to find a way out of the tunnels. I didn't know how long my flashlight would last, but I didn't dare turn it off for fear of not seeing where I was going and what I might run into. The door was locked tight. I banged on it, but to no avail, and it hurt my hands to do so. I didn't want to bang with the flashlight because I thought I might break it. Thank God, I had my new jacket on because it was cold in the tunnels. Finally I decided my only option was to go to the other end of the tunnel to see if there was a way out. I knew it was a long way, but what else could I do?

This tunnel was supposed to come out somewhere in the next town, which was miles away. I had no choice; I had to make a try for it. The smell was terrible, but I could get through that. It was the spiders and anything else that was lurking down there that I wasn't sure of.

I would just have to be brave like Father. Could I be as brave as him? I didn't know. I had no food or water, and I was cold. The tunnel was fairly wide, at least for me, and it was high enough so that I didn't have to walk stooped over. At least that was something. The floor was dirt, but it was hard packed and easy to walk on.

The first problem I encountered was a pile of rocks and bricks laying on the floor. I shined my flashlight on the roof of the tunnel and saw a large hole formed when the debris fell. That meant that the tunnel was old and could cave in anywhere. I wondered if it had caved in somewhere else ahead and if I might come to a dead end. There was no turning back now. I had gone perhaps two or three hundred yards, but I wasn't sure.

I tried counting steps, but got distracted and lost count. I heard a squeaking noise and there it was – a rat as big as a cat! I threw a rock at it, and it ran down the tunnel. I wondered how many more of them there were. But the rat was a good sign – if there were rats in the tunnel that meant there was a way out.

The tunnel curved a little to the right, but there seemed to be only one way to go. I didn't see any splits in it, thank God. I went on and on, but didn't encounter any more rats. There were some spider webs, but I didn't see any spiders. I don't know which was worse: seeing spider webs without spiders or with them. Most of the webs seemed to be along the sides of the tunnel, so that was something. It was easy to avoid them.

I sure didn't want to sleep in the tunnel so I hurried. I wondered how long it would take me to get to the other end. What if there was a door and it was locked too? That kind of thinking didn't help so I forced myself to stop and just focus on getting to the end. I thought about running, but that was too dangerous because of all the debris on the floor. What if there was a hole in the floor? I watched where I stepped.

I thought I heard more rats up ahead. Maybe they heard me coming and would run away; yes, that's what they would do – they'd run away from me. I'd yell and scare them. I remembered reading once about someone yelling in the mountains and causing an avalanche. I wondered if yelling could cause a cave-in. I decided not to yell.

I picked up some rocks and put them in my pocket just in case and discovered candy. I must have put some in there and forgot about it. There were six pieces, all wrapped. Energy in case I needed it. My flashlight was working well, but for how long?

I had to keep moving fast. I could see only a few feet ahead of me with the flashlight. Its beam was strong, but not strong enough to shine way out ahead like I would have preferred. The sides of the tunnel were wet and so was the floor. Water had gotten in the tunnel from some place, but where? All sorts of thoughts ran through my head – like what if a wall of water suddenly raced down the tunnel and trapped me, or what if I come to a dead end with no place to go?

I stopped those thoughts and concentrated on getting out of the tunnel.

Meanwhile, back in town, Inspector Edwards had put out a bulletin to the neighboring towns to be on the lookout for me. Mother had gotten a hold of Father and he was on his way back to Soham. Even Nancy was looking for me. Mother was almost at her wits' end. She was so upset that a doctor suggested that she lay down for a few hours. He recommended that she take a sedative, but Mother refused to take medicine of any kind. When Mother was young a family member had taken some pills that made him or her sick and ever since she has refused to take medicine of any kind.

When Father came home his first suggestion was to search the house again. Inspector Edwards told him that it was searched already, but Father insisted on searching it again. So Father, Mother and Nancy began a thorough search of the house. Mother wouldn't stay in bed as Father and the doctor had suggested. Father found Tom Walsh and demanded that every room be opened, even the apartments that weren't being used. Mr. Walsh agreed, and they looked everywhere, but found nothing.

"What about the tunnels?" Father asked.

"Inspector Edwards already looked down there and said all the doors were locked," Mother said.

"But what if someone locked William in the tunnel?" Father asked.

"Why would someone do that?" Mother inquired.

"The Bible is missing, and the whole town probably knows that William saw the killer leaving the scene of the crime. Need I say more?" Father exclaimed.

"Oh no! You don't think someone would hurt William do you?" Mother implored.

"I don't know what to think right now," Father said. "All I know is that William is missing and Inspector Edwards has no suspect for the murder. That means whoever did it is still on the loose."

"Oh, God, please, no," Mother cried.

"We have to face reality, Mary, and you know it. I believe that William is all right. He's a smart boy and can take care of himself," Father said. "We've taught him how to handle himself in situations that require thinking."

"But, Henry, he's only 9 years old. How can he…" Mother started to say.

"Now, just get a hold of yourself, Mary," Father interrupted. "He'll be all right. We've got to keep on looking. I'm going to get Mr. Walsh to unlock the door to the basement and the tunnels and have a look around. You stay here for now. It'll be better if I look alone."

So Father and Mr. Walsh went into the basement and then into the tunnel.

"The doors were locked, and he couldn't have locked them from the inside," Mr. Walsh said

"But what if someone locked him in?" Father asked.

"Why would someone want to do that? Besides I had the keys right here all the time," Mr. Walsh said.

"Did you have the keys on you, or were they hanging behind the door?" Father inquired.

"They were hanging behind the door where they always are," Mr. Walsh replied.

"Then how do you know if someone didn't come down here, take the keys and lock William in the tunnel?" Father asked.

"Well, he's not here," Mr. Walsh replied emphatically.

"What about the door to the long tunnel?" Father asked.

"That door hasn't been open in years," Mr. Walsh replied.

"Do you have the key for it?" Father asked.

"Yes, it's right here, but I think the door is stuck. I've never been able to open it," Mr. Walsh said.

So Mr. Walsh and Father went back upstairs. If they had only looked at the door to the long tunnel they might have seen that it had been opened recently and they might have found me.

It seemed that I had been in this tunnel for days, but I knew it had only been hours. I was getting tired; I needed to rest. I was too scared to lie down because of the water and rats and spiders; I kept going.

Suddenly I heard something. It sounded like rushing water up ahead. After going about 50 feet I began to hear it more clearly. It was the sound of water, but where was it coming from?

I shined my flashlight all around, but still couldn't see the source of the sound. I hoped it wasn't rushing toward me. All I needed was rushing water filling up the tunnel. No, that wasn't it. It was getting closer. There it was – the water. It seemed to be running across the tunnel from one side to the other. It was coming from under one side and going out the other.

Whew! I figured it was an underground stream. Too bad it didn't have a larger opening on either side because I might have been able to crawl out. I used my hands to sip some of the water. It was really cold and refreshing. I didn't know how clean it was, but it was wet and cold and tasted good; that was all I cared about at the moment. I wished I had something to put the water in, but I didn't.

I stepped over the little stream and continued on my journey. I didn't know how long I had been in the tunnel, but it must have been a long time because I was tired and hungry. I ate a piece of candy and it tasted good. I had five left and was determined to save them as long as I could. Was I going to die in the tunnel? No, I wouldn't accept that. I would make it out somehow.

I thought of Billy. Would she miss me if I were gone? If I died would she come to my funeral? My whole family would be there. I could see Mother crying with her arm around Nancy. Father would be there in his Air Force uniform, standing straight and tall without a tear in his eye because men don't cry. No, no, I had to think of something else, but what?

Goldie came to mind. She was such a nice puppy. She would come in my room and sleep on my bed all curled up in a little ball of fluff. Mother didn't like her getting on the bed, but I would let her come up if Mother wasn't around. I always had a treat for Goldie, and she licked my hand as if to say thank you. I was getting sleepy. It must be nighttime by now. I had to find a place to rest.

My family had a lonely dinner that night. They would continue the search the next day.

The next morning there was a knock at the front door. Father answered the door and there stood Inspector Edwards.

"Come in, Inspector," Father said. "Would you like some coffee?"

"No thank you, I just had my tea. I came over to tell you that I'm calling a town meeting this morning at 10. I'm going to try to organize the search, and I have some other reasons for the meeting," Inspector Edwards told Father.

"What other reasons?" Father asked.

"Well, let's just say that I want to see who shows up and who doesn't," Inspector Edwards said.

"Oh, I see. Maybe you think the killer won't be there?" Father suggested.

"Perhaps, but maybe it isn't who doesn't show up, but who does," Inspector Edwards replied.

"I'm not sure I get your drift," Father said.

"My drift? Oh, yes, quite right, my drift. Your American expressions are new to me," Inspector Edwards said. "I think it might help if we see who comes, and it won't hurt to get everyone more organized. I feel that if we coordinated our search we might be more effective, don't you think?"

"Maybe, but I'm not sure we're looking in the right places. I still want to get inside that long tunnel," Father said. "I feel that has something to do with where William is, and I can't get rid of the thought."

"Mr. Walsh told me that the door to the long tunnel hasn't been opened in years," Inspector Edwards said.

"Yes, he told me that too, but I don't believe him," Father responded.

"You think he's lying?" the inspector asked.

"Maybe, just maybe," Father replied. "He wants this house you know. He told my wife that he tried to buy it from Rev. Holder."

"I thought Mr. Styles wanted the house," the inspector said.

"That's right, he wants it, too," Father replied.

"It seems like everyone wants this old house," Inspector Edwards said. "My understanding is that if Rev. Holder died that put this house back into the hands of Mr. Styles because his family owned it originally and gave it to Rev. Holder, but only for as long as he lived. It seems that Mr. Style's family didn't want him to have the house, for some unknown reason, and they thought that Rev. Holder would live a long time. So they gave it over to him. However, the will specifically states that the house reverts back to Mr. Styles when and if Rev. Holder ever died."

"But doesn't that mean Mr. Styles is not a prime suspect because Rev. Holder didn't die. Poor Mr. Cox died instead," Father said.

"It would, but there is one problem with that logic," the inspector said.

"What problem?" Father asked.

"The fact that Mr. Styles has a good alibi for where he was on Christmas Day. I'd already thought of your idea, but his alibi is pretty tight," the inspector added.

"Where was he?" Father asked.

"He was in Newmarket visiting his relatives for Christmas," Inspector Edwards said.

"But isn't that a few miles from here?" Father asked.

"Yes, it is," the inspector said.

"Well, if it's just a few miles from here, what's to keep Mr. Styles from slipping away from his family for the length of time it would take to come here to try and kill Rev. Holder, steal the Bible and get back to Newmarket before anyone knew he had left? And when he found Mr. Cox in the office with the Bible he killed him instead, or maybe killed him accidentally," Father said with excitement.

"You have a point there. Yes, you do. I do suppose it's possible for him to drive over here and get back without taking much time. Maybe I'll have another talk with Mr. Styles," the inspector said thoughtfully.

"Let's wait to see if he shows up at the meeting first," Father suggested.

"Good idea, yes, that's what we'll do," Inspector Edwards agreed. "Oh, by the way, you might be interested to know that Mr. Styles is not the only one who had a motive to kill Rev. Holder, but remember, he's not the one who is dead."

"I guess anyone could have a motive. They knew he had a very valuable Bible and that was motive enough wasn't it?" Father asked.

"That's right, but my investigation has turned up some interesting things about the people in this town as well," the inspector responded.

"Like what?" Father asked.

"Well, for one thing Miss Stone, the candy store owner, used to be engaged to Rev. Holder. Evidently he left her at the altar in 1939, and she has hated him ever since," he said.

"You're kidding!" Father exclaimed.

"No, and that's not all. There are some other people in this town who want to leave, but don't have the money to go where they want in the style they want," Inspector Edwards continued. "I can think of several people who have the motive to kill for the Bible and for the money it would bring."

"I wish I had never found that stupid Bible," Father muttered.

"That's all water under the bridge right now; there is nothing we can do about that. You found it and that's that. What we need to do now is find William," the inspector said.

"Don't you have any clues from the crime scene?" Father asked.

"No, not one. No fingerprints, except for Rev. Holder's and Mr. Cox's. No weapon, no nothing," was the inspector's answer.

The night had been very long for me. I think I fell asleep sometime after I sat down for a few minutes. I awoke cold, stiff and hungry. I had eaten another piece of candy before I dozed off, so I had just four pieces left.

I ate another for strength; it helped. I was so thirsty I could have drunk a gallon of water. I wished I had some of the water from the stream. On the bright side, the night hadn't been too cold because I wasn't frozen. Maybe the tunnel insulated me from the cold outside.

It was time to get moving. At least I hadn't been bothered by rats during the night. I was glad I remembered to turn off my flashlight or it would have been dead for sure. I wasn't sure what possessed me to turn it off because I was really scared of the dark. Maybe it was an angel. Mother always said angels protect us. I'd never seen one, but Mother says they are real so they must be. Mother says each of us has a guardian angel who looks out for us all the time.

"Well, angel, if you're out there, I hope you are ready to get me out of here," I said to myself.

I turned on my flashlight, and it worked fine. I could see up ahead for about 20 feet. This entire tunnel looked the same to me: cold, dark, smelly and dirty.

The rats must have heard me coming and ran away because I hadn't seen one since yesterday. Yesterday; that sounded funny. Had I been in the tunnel that long? I wondered what my parents were doing. I figured Mother was probably very upset. I hoped they would look for me soon. Surely someone would think to look in this tunnel.

As I walked my stomach grumbled hungrily. I could have used some of Mother's pancakes. She made the best pancakes in the world. I'd usually eat five or six of them, all stacked high with butter and syrup. Better to think of something else; thoughts of food did not quiet my stomach.

I wondered how far I went yesterday. Did I go a mile or more? Maybe I did; I didn't know. How much farther was it to the next town?

"Just keep walking," I told myself, "just keep walking."

Then what sounded like a train howled through the tunnel. The ground shook. I looked above me … oh no!

CHAPTER 6
Trapped!

The town meeting went off without a hitch. Inspector Edwards told everyone that the priority for today was to find me. He wanted a concentrated search starting at the house grounds and fanning out from there. He expected everyone to help. He reminded everyone that if one of their children were missing they would want the same thing. He put the constable in charge of one search group and Father in charge of another. He would be in charge of the third group.

Each group was given a specific search area; everyone would meet at the center of town when they completed the search of their area.

He told the searchers not to leave any stone unturned when looking – to open every cabinet or old box or shed, to look behind every shrub and every tree. He was being somewhat dramatic, but they got the point. All the townspeople showed up for the meeting to the dismay of Father and the inspector. This was going to be harder to solve than they thought. With so many people having a motive, how was Inspector Edwards ever going to figure it out?

Inspector Edwards was looking for me, but he was also kept his eye open for the Gutenberg Bible. Whoever had it had hidden it well. The inspector was turning the town upside down looking for it, but so far with no luck. It was either out of town somewhere or hidden very well. He didn't believe the murderer would try to sell it so soon. Whoever had it would have to bide their time until things cooled off and then probably take it to Europe and try to sell it there.

Father's group started at the house and worked their way through the church grounds. This took a while because old churches like this one, which dated back to the 10th century, had so many places one could hide that it took hours just to search the building itself, let alone the basement and the grounds.

From the church they worked their way down one of the local streets, stopping at every house to ask if they could search it. Inspector Edwards had told the town folk that this would happen and to expect it. He asked everyone to be cooperative and if they weren't he could get search warrants for every house if necessary. Warrants weren't needed because everyone did cooperate, and most people in town were searching themselves anyway. Every house was searched from top to bottom. This took most of the day, but to no avail. No Bible and no William. They were back to square one and didn't know what to do next.

Meanwhile, I could hardly breathe. It felt like a ton of bricks had fallen on me and that's about what happened. My arm was hurting really badly. I wondered if it was broken. I managed to crawl out from under the rocks. I don't know how long I was under there, but it must have been for some time. My flashlight was missing. I started to dig in the rocks, feeling my way, looking for the light, but no light. My arm was throbbing. I couldn't move it very well. Mother said if your arm was broken you couldn't move your fingers or at least it would hurt a lot. Well, I could move my fingers, but it hurt to do so.

I moved rocks as best as I could in the pitch darkness. Suddenly there was a light, a small glimmer coming from about 6 or 7 inches under the rubble. It had to be my flashlight. I dug some more and reached it. It still worked. What a miracle!

When the ceiling collapsed I must have put my arm up over my head just as the rocks came down because that would account for my arm getting hurt. At least it wasn't my head! My angel had protected me again. I thanked him, and then I was off down the tunnel.

This time I turned the light toward the roof from time to time just to be safe. If I heard any more rumbling, I was going to fall down and cover myself as best I could. I ate another piece of candy. Now I had three pieces left. I was glad it was the long-lasting, chewy candy. The first chance I got I would thank Miss Stone!

The tunnel seemed to narrow a little, at least it looked that way. I heard squeaking again. Oh no, more rats! They were up ahead someplace; I could hear them. I had a good supply of rocks. I threw some down the tunnel, but I couldn't see anything. At least my throwing arm wasn't hurt.

Up above, the search ended around five in the evening when it grew too dark to see. Inspector Edwards didn't want to call it off but he had to. Some of the townspeople had good lights and wanted to continue searching, so Inspector Edwards let them go ahead on with the search. Most of the people went home to their nice warm houses and their dinners.

Mother and Father went home, too. They couldn't eat or sleep, but they went home anyway. There were many tears that night in my house. Father comforted Mother and Nancy.

"We'll look again tomorrow. I won't stop until I find William," Father declared.

Mother and Nancy laid beside Father on the couch in the living room. Nancy soon fell asleep, but Mother just laid there, crying softly.

"Don't worry about William, Mary, he's a good boy, and God will protect him," Father said reassuringly. Father's statement gave Mother hope. They prayed all night for me. Tomorrow would be a new day.

I know I feel asleep after I sat down to rest, but I don't know when. I had lost all track of time in the darkness. I woke up and tried to turn my flashlight on, but it was on. Oh no, I had left it on all night, and it had finally burned out. Now, what was I going to do?

I felt a real sense of panic, and I began to cry.

"Men don't cry," Father always said, but I wasn't a man yet. I was only 9. Now I was in total darkness with no flashlight to show me the way. I was tired, hungry and my arm hurt badly. It was so stiff I could hardly move it. Was it broken? Maybe, but what did it matter? I was probably going to die in the tunnel. I never felt so scared and alone in all my life.

I ate a piece of candy. Two left. I was starving; what did saving them matter? So I ate the last two pieces. It sure tasted good, but I was so thirsty that my tongue was swollen.

I sat in the pitch dark thinking of food. I wished I could have some of Mother's special French toast. She made it so the edges of the bread were crispy. I don't believe there is any better French toast anywhere. Add some butter, just a tad of cinnamon and then a little syrup.

I had to stop thinking of food. I needed to figure out how I was going to get out of this place. I didn't think I could move if I wanted to. I was so stiff I felt like a piece of leather that had gotten wet and then dried out. Then I heard a terrible rumble. No not again …

While I suffered through another roof collapse in the tunnel, my family awoke.

Nancy ran into the kitchen yelling for Mother and Father.

"There's no flashlight on William's night table by his bed," she shouted. "I was looking for something and needed a flashlight, so I went into William's room to borrow his but it's not there."

"What are you getting at Nancy?" Mother asked.

"Don't you see? William only keeps that flashlight by his bed so he can look at the spiders during the night to see where they are. He never moves it unless he takes it with him someplace," Nancy cried excitedly.

"That's right!" Mother gasped.

"So you think he went somewhere where he needed his flashlight?" Father asked.

"That's what I think," Nancy quickly answered.

"It must be the tunnels!" Mother shouted.

"I'm going to get those keys from Tom Walsh and go down there and search. Nancy, you go find Inspector Edwards and tell him what we're doing," Father yelled, racing for the door.

"Wait, I'll go with you, Henry!" Mother called after him.

While Father went to find Mr. Walsh, Nancy set out to find Inspector Edwards. He wasn't hard to find because he always had tea and biscuits for breakfast at the Boar's Head Inn. Nancy found him there and told him what Father and Mother were going to do.

"I must be losing my mind. What have I been thinking? I know a man who has bloodhounds who can help us search. Why didn't I think of that before? I'll call and ask him to get his dogs over here as fast as possible," the inspector responded.

"Thanks, Inspector. I'll see you over at the house," Nancy said and then ran all the way home.

Mother and Father already had flashlights and warm coats and were looking for the keys to the tunnel.

"They're not here!" Father exclaimed. "Tom must have them. Mary, you wait here, and I'll be back in a minute with the keys."

"I'm not waiting down here in this dark basement without you," Mother answered quickly. "I'm coming with you."

"Oh, all right, come on then," said Father, giving in.

As they went back upstairs, they ran into Nancy coming down. She told them that Inspector Edwards was getting bloodhounds to help.

"They'll need a piece of William's clothing," Mother said. "I'll go and get it and bring it with us while you look for Mr. Walsh."

Inspector Edwards called Mr. Hodges. He had bloodhounds that the inspector had used before. Inspector Edwards had used Mr. Hodges' dogs once to solve a missing person case and they had proven invaluable.

"I just hope we're in time," the inspector said to himself.

Mr. Hodges arrived in an old black pickup truck with three of his best hounds laying in the back.

Quickly Inspector Edwards led them over to St. Andrew's House. Introductions were made.

"Mr. and Mrs. Allen, this is Mr. Hodges. If his dogs can't find William no one can," the inspector said.

The dogs sniffed some of the clothing that Mother had brought them. Suddenly they began howling loudly.

"They've got the scent already!" the inspector shouted.

The dogs were loosed and immediately dashed through the house and headed straight for the basement.

Inspector Edwards met Father in the hallway leading to the kitchen.

"I can't find Tom Walsh," Father told him.

"Do we need him?" the inspector asked.

"He has the keys to the tunnels. They're usually here on this hook behind the kitchen door, but they're gone and Tom's nowhere to be found. I can't find Mrs. Walsh either," Father replied.

"If he's not here why would he take the keys with him?" the inspector mused.

"I don't know, but I'm going to find out," Father declared.

Meanwhile, the dogs were sniffing at the basement door, so Father opened it.

The dogs ran down the stairs toward the tunnels howling loudly.

"He must be down this way!" Mr. Hodges yelled. "Do you have any tools that we can use to get that door open?"

"That door is solid English oak," Father replied. "We'd need a bulldozer to get it open."

The dogs scratched at the door something fierce and howled so loudly it echoed throughout the house.

"Calm those dogs down while we figure out how to open that door," the inspector said loudly.

"Once they get the scent I can't get them to leave it," Mr. Hodges explained.

"Well, do something!" the inspector demanded.

So Mr. Hodges put the dogs back on their leashes and escorted them upstairs. But what a job he had doing it! They fought him every step of the way. They had my scent, and they were determined to find me.

"If we have to we can cut the door down," Inspector Edwards suggested.

"Do something!" Mother cried. "William could be in there dying!"

"We'll get him out, love, just trust us," the inspector said.

"I've got it!" cried Mr. Hodges snapping, his fingers. "I've got a cable hoist on the front of my four-wheel-drive truck. It's very long. It might reach from the front door down here."

"What if you park in the back and we pull it through the kitchen window?" Father suggested.

"That's it! Let's try it! I'll go move it around back right now," said Mr. Hodges, leaving quickly.

He moved his vehicle to the back of the house, brought the cable in through the window and down the stairs. It reached all the way to the tunnel door. He attached it to the door and quickly started up his engine to give more power to the hoist. The solid oak door creaked and cracked, and then split open with a crash. Father, Mother, Inspector Edwards and the bloodhounds surged through the doorway into the tunnels. The bloodhounds immediately ran to the door that went to the long tunnel and began to scratch at the edge of it.

"He must be in there. Look. This door has been opened recently; see the drag marks on the floor," Father pointed out.

The cable would not reach to that door; they were stuck again.

"I have some rope in the back of my truck. Let me attach it to the cable and see if it will reach to the door," Mr. Hodges suggested.

They attached the rope to the cable and then to the door of the long tunnel. Mr. Hodges started the cable motor and it started pulling but the door would not budge. The rope stretched and the cable motor strained, but to no avail. Mr. Hodges tried backing up his vehicle but the rope just broke.

They tied it and tried again. This time the cable tore the window sash out completely. They were ready to admit defeat.

"Lord, please help us," Mother whispered as Nancy came running.

"I found the keys! I found the keys!" she shouted.

"Where did you find them?" Father asked, grabbing for the keys.

"They were in Mr. Walsh's old coat that he leaves by the door to his apartment," Nancy said.

"What on earth possessed you to look there?" the inspector asked.

"I just thought that maybe he left the keys in his coat because he wears that coat all the time when he's working around the house," Nancy replied.

"Good thinking," the inspector said. "Now let's try those keys."

After several tries the keys opened the door and the bloodhounds shot through it like bullets from a gun. Their baying echoed throughout the tunnel.

"So much for a door that cannot be opened!" Father said.

Inspector Edwards, Father and Mr. Hodges followed the dogs as fast as they could. Nancy and Mother decided it would be best if they stayed behind.

The group reached the first cave-in quickly and then the little stream. The bloodhounds ran through the stream and caught the scent again. They were too far ahead of Father and the others to see them with the flashlights, but they could hear them all right. Soon the dogs reached a dead end. The entire tunnel was blocked by fallen rocks. The dogs were howling and scratching at the rocks when the others caught up with them.

It had taken quite sometime for them to reach the dogs. Everyone was out of breath from running so far so fast. If they called my name I was unaware of it, because the second cave-in knocked me out.

Father, being a strong man, began picking up rocks and throwing them behind him. Some of the stones were quite heavy, but he could lift heavy weights. His high school wrestling days (he had been a state champ for his Illinois high school) and time spent working in a steel foundry paid off in this situation. The three men worked quickly, digging through the rubble. All the time they were digging the dogs howled and scratched. Mr. Hodges said this was a good sign and that someone was probably still alive behind all this debris.

Finally, after seemingly digging all morning, they found me. Inspector Edwards found a shoe first and was glad to find a foot attached to it. When they got the rocks off me I was still breathing, but unconscious. Father carried me all the way back through the tunnel.

I woke up in the local hospital with Mother, Father, Nancy and Inspector Edwards all looking at me.

"Can I have some water please?" I croaked.

"He's awake!" Nancy shouted.

"Oh, my baby!" Mother cried.

"You gave us quite a scare, William, my lad," the inspector said.

"Someone locked me in there," I said. "I think it was the killer."

"What makes you say that?" Father asked.

"Because I smelled that same fish smell just before they closed the door and locked me in. Hey, why is my arm in a cast?" I cried.

"Your arm is broken," Mother told me. "You also had a slight concussion, but the doctor said you'll be all right."

"When those stones fell on me I thought I was gone for sure. I'm really hungry. Can I have something to eat?" I asked.

"Just some soup and a few crackers for now, William; doctor's orders," Mother answered.

"Can I see you both out in the hall for a second?" the inspector quietly asked my parents.

While Nancy fed me the soup, Mother and Father went out in the hall to talk with Inspector Edwards.

"I'm going to post a constable outside William's door for now. If the killer tried once to get rid of William he might try to do it again," he said.

"Oh no!" Mother exclaimed, turning pale.

"He'll be all right. He has to stay in here for a few days for observation, so we'll keep a guard on the door 24 hours a day," the inspector promised.

"I'm staying right here with him, too," Mother declared.

"I have to get back to the base, Mary, because there is something I have to check on. What about Nancy?" Father asked.

"She can stay here, too. Besides, I'd feel better if they were both where I could keep my eye on them," Mother's replied.

"Don't worry about your family, Mr. Allen. I'll make sure they are taken care of," Inspector Edwards assured Father.

So Father went back to Lakenheath-Mildenhall. What we didn't know at the time was that Father had contacts within British intelligence, so he made a few phone calls. Mother and Nancy stayed with me at the hospital. We played rummy and talked. They asked me all about my ordeal in the tunnel. The local newspaper even sent someone to interview me. They said someone from the BBC might come by as well.

I was becoming a celebrity at the age of 9! My arm didn't hurt, but it itched like crazy. I had a bandage on my head and several small bandages on my hands and legs, but all in all I had survived a terrible ordeal. People from town came by and brought me toys, candy and all sorts of good stuff. Everything and everybody was checked thoroughly by the constable outside my door. He was under strict orders from Inspector Edwards not to let anyone in who might have a weapon of any kind. He also checked every item they brought me for gifts.

The BBC did send a reporter to interview me. I told him about my ordeal in complete detail, including the rats! He had a cameraman and everything. It was very exciting. I saw myself on TV later that day. I wondered if Billy saw me on TV. More than that, I wondered if the killer saw me, too. If he or she did, which we were hoping happened, the trap was laid.

Inspector Edwards had asked my parents if they would agree to an idea he had. He proposed that I make statements to the news that I knew who the killer was, that an arrest was imminent and that I was prepared to testify in court when I got out of the hospital.

He hoped that the killer would hear this and make a run for it.

Mother suggested that the killer might decide to try to kill me again and that it was too risky, but Father and Inspector Edwards assured her that I would be safe. She reluctantly agreed to their scheme.

So now I was the bait. I told the press that I knew who the killer was and that I could identify the person. This was a bold move since I really couldn't identify anyone. It was a long shot, but hopefully it would pay off.

I got out of the hospital a few days later. Nothing happened while I was hospitalized and this upset the inspector. I guess he was hoping someone would try to kill me again. What a lovely thought! I was sure he had his motives, but I was glad nothing happened and so was Mother. Either the killer ran for it with the Bible or he was being sly and laying low.

The case was no further along than it was the day the inspector started investigating it. This was an embarrassment to Inspector Edwards and to Scotland Yard. But he wasn't giving up. On the contrary, he was more determined than ever to find the killer and the Gutenberg Bible. Whoever had the Bible was undoubtedly the killer. So Inspector Edwards redoubled his efforts and began interviewing Soham residents again, much to their dismay.

Mother and I went on an important errand to Miss Stone's house. The constable kept us company on orders from Inspector Edwards. We wanted to know just what diet Miss Stone had been using for her Corgis. She had mentioned something to Mother when she got the puppy about a special diet. Miss Stone's house was just behind her candy store. It was very neat and tidy with pretty blue curtains made of lace in the windows. Her house was small but comfortable. The furniture looked old, but I guess she liked it. She had a nice fireplace with a picture of Queen

Elizabeth above the mantle. She had a large grandfather clock in the corner that chimed every 15 minutes. It was so loud I wondered how she slept at night.

Miss Stone had four Corgis. She told us that Corgis were the favorite dogs of the queen and that's why she had them. The funniest thing was that I smelled that same fish smell that I had smelled before in the church, at the funeral and in the tunnel. I suddenly got a very queasy feeling inside my stomach. I must have looked sick because Mother asked me if I was all right. I told her that I was and that I'd tell her later about it. She accepted my answer, and we continued our visit.

Miss Stone was very hospitable. She brought us tea and small cakes – the kind I liked from Mrs. Moore's bakery. We had tea and talked about nothing in particular when out of the blue Miss Stone asked if Inspector Edwards had found the Bible yet. We told her that we didn't think so, but he was searching for it all over town.

Then she asked me a strange question.

"William, I understand that you think you can identify the killer," she said.

"That's right," I said.

"Well, who is it?" she asked.

"I can't say Miss Stone because Inspector Edwards asked me not to at this time," I replied.

It was the only thing I could think of to say. I was caught off guard when she asked the question.

Mother changed the subject quickly and asked about the puppy's diet. Miss Stone took us into her kitchen where she showed us how she mixed their food. She combined some slightly cooked ground beef with small amounts of fish. That was the smell! Now I could smell it clearly. My thoughts began to race in my head, and I could see that Mother was thinking the same thing. We made a hasty excuse about some shopping we had to do and left.

Once we were clear of Miss Stone's house Mother asked me if that was the fish smell I had smelled.

"You were thinking what I was thinking, weren't you, Mother?" I asked.

"I sure was. Do you suppose Miss Stone killed Mr. Cox to get the Bible?" she asked.

"I don't know, but I need to tell Inspector Edwards about this right away," I answered.

We found Inspector Edwards having lunch at the Boar's Head Inn. We told him about the fish smell and Miss Stone. He said he would look into it right away. We went home and Inspector Edwards went straight over to Miss Stone's house. He found her in her candy store.

"Miss Stone, may I speak with you for a moment please?" he asked.

"Why, of course, Inspector. What is it you want?" she asked.

"Could you tell me again where you were on Christmas Day?" he asked.

"As I told you before, Inspector, I was at home by myself. I live alone you know," she said.

"Would you care to tell me why Rev. Holder didn't show up at your intended wedding in 1939?" he asked.

"Oh, how did you know about that?" she asked shakily.

"The point is I know about it. Would you please answer the question?" Edwards said in his firmest police tone.

"I don't see where the relevance is to this investigation; he's not the one who is dead," Miss Stone replied sharply.

"I'll be the judge of that if you don't mind," replied Inspector Edwards with impatience.

"We were engaged to be married, and he decided to become a minister instead. That's all there is to it, Inspector," she said.

"You mean to tell me that you didn't hate him for what he had done?" Inspector Edwards asked.

"You mean enough to kill him, don't you? Why don't you just say so? Yes, I hated him for it, but not enough to murder him or anyone else," Miss Stone said, her eyes snapping.

"Not even when you heard that he had a very valuable Bible?" he asked.

"Yes, I heard about the Bible, but what's that got to do with it?" she parried.

"It has everything to do with it, Miss Stone. You hated Rev. Holder for leaving you at the altar. Then when you found out he had this Bible, you decided to kill him for it, but Mr. Cox was there instead and you ended up killing him. Your plan was to leave town, sell the Bible and live happily ever after," Inspector Edwards accused.

"That's not true, I didn't kill anybody!" she cried.

"Then you won't mind if I search your house, will you?" he asked.

"Be my guest, Inspector. I'll even give you the key, but try not to let my dogs out if you please," she said.

So Inspector Edwards took the key from Miss Stone and went behind the candy store to her house. After being greeted by the dogs, and nearly getting bitten, he began his search. He locked the dogs up in the kitchen so he could look around without being bothered by them. His search was well worth it because he found some blood on one of her shoes in the closet. At least it looked like blood; he would have to get it analyzed. He took the shoe and left, sending the shoe to London by train immediately. He told the conductor it was a Scotland Yard priority package. It didn't take long for the lab results to come back. It was blood all right – Mr. Cox's blood. The call went directly to the inn as soon as the results were known.

Inspector Edwards went right to the candy store and arrested Miss Stone for the murder of Mr. Cox.

News travels fast in a small town. Everyone knew about Miss Stone's arrest almost as fast as it had happened. Inspector Edwards put the fish smell together with her hatred of the reverend and the blood on her shoe. He was going to make this arrest stick.

Miss Stone had a motive, no alibi and there was some evidence that she was at the scene of the crime. Hopefully she would cave in during the interrogation, admit the murder and disclose the whereabouts of the Bible.

When we heard the news of Miss Stone's arrest we were at first relieved, but we were sorry as well. What a sad story. She seemed like such a nice lady. What would happen to her candy store and her dogs?

Those were the things on my mind. I knew I was partly responsible for her arrest. I felt badly about it – like I had caused it to happen in the first place. I knew I had smelled that fish smell on three occasions and then again at her house. But she was such a nice lady! The blood on her shoe was the final straw. There didn't seem to be any way she could explain her way out of that one. I wondered where she hid the Bible. I guessed that would come out in the investigation.

Mother was relieved beyond all measure. She was just happy that someone had been arrested, even if it was Miss Stone. Yes, she had given us the puppy and been kind to us, but if she was the murderer then she deserved to suffer the consequences.

Inspector Edwards escorted Miss Stone to London on the train. This time he had evidence that would identify her as the killer. When they arrived at Scotland Yard he took her to be booked for the murder. She had her fingerprints taken along with her picture. Then she was taken to the interrogation room, where Inspector Edwards and one of his colleagues questioned her about the murder. They hoped to get a confession from her.

"Now, Miss Stone, would you like to change your story from the one you told me in Soham about the murder of Mr. Cox?" Inspector Edwards asked.

The interrogation was being taped and watched by other Scotland Yard homicide experts from behind a two-way mirror.

"I told you inspector; I didn't kill anybody," Miss Stone replied.

"Can you explain why we found blood on your shoe that matches Mr. Cox' perfectly?" he continued.

"Yes, I can," she said, as she began to cry. "I wanted to get back at Rev. Holder for what he had done to me. I thought if I could get into his office and steal the Gutenberg Bible that he would be blamed for it. I thought it being Christmas Day and all that he would not be there, so I went in the church and into his office, but Mr. Cox was already dead on the floor. I ran away. I guess that's when I got blood on my shoe."

"Why didn't you report his death to the authorities?" the inspector asked.

"I was scared, and I figured that I would be blamed because everyone knew how I hated Rev. Holder," she replied, continuing to weep.

"Did you see the Bible?" Inspector Edwards asked.

"No," she said, "it wasn't there that I could see, but I wasn't really looking for it once I saw that man was dead."

"How did you know he was dead? Did you check his breathing?" he asked.

"Yes, I did and I guess that's how I got close to the blood on the floor, but I didn't kill him. I didn't!" Miss Stone exclaimed.

"Do you know where the Bible is, Miss Stone?" Inspector Edwards continued.

"No, I told you it wasn't there. The real killer must have taken it," she answered.

"When did this happen?" the inspector asked.

"How do I know? Sometime before I got there," she replied.

"Can you tell us what time it was when you got there?" he asked.

"Around 8:45 I guess. I'm not sure," she said.

"How did you leave the church?" Inspector Edwards continued.

"I ran out the back way," she said.

"Were you carrying anything with you?" he went on.

"Just the bag I brought with me to put the Bible in," Miss Stone said.

"It's an interesting story Miss Stone, but I'm afraid it doesn't wash with me. You had every motive to kill Rev. Holder and you ended up killing poor Mr. Cox instead. Then you took the Bible as a reward for your years of torment. Isn't that right?" the inspector pressed.

"No, no, it isn't! I didn't kill him! Why won't you believe me?" she sobbed.

"We don't believe you, Miss Stone, because your story won't hold up in court. You had the motive, and even though you ended up killing another man it doesn't matter, it's still murder no matter how you figure it. You have no alibi for your whereabouts on Christmas Day. The Bible is still missing and unless you can tell us where it is I'm afraid you're going to be here for some time, probably a lifetime," Inspector Edwards said.

"I don't know where the Bible is! I've told you I found him dead when I got there, and I didn't see the Bible!" Miss Stone cried.

"How did you first hear about the Bible, Miss Stone?" Inspector Edwards persisted.

"I ... I don't remember. I think William came into my store and told me about it. What's going to happen to my store? What about my dogs? My whole life is in that store," she said.

"Your store has been locked up and there is a sign on the front to stay away. Your dogs were taken to the local vet, where he is keeping them. They're safe," the inspector assured.

"But he won't give them their proper meal. They have to have their special diet that I make for them out of cooked ground beef and fish," Miss Stone went on.

"Did you say fish?" the inspector asked quickly.

"Yes, why?" she asked.

"Nothing, just don't worry about your dogs, Miss Stone. Where you're going I think you won't be seeing your dogs anymore," he said.

They questioned Miss Stone for three hours and finally took her crying back to her cell. Inspector Edwards seemed worried about the fish that she fed her dogs, but he couldn't understand why. The case seemed to be solved. Now the rest was up to the courts and a jury. Inspector Edwards had one more thought, and he was going to pursue it to see where it led.

CHAPTER 7

Some Fishy Business

Life in Soham returned to normal for my family. Father was back at the base, Nancy and I were back in school, and Mother was calm for the first time in weeks.

It was really too bad for Miss Stone. I never would have thought she was a murderer, but people can surprise you. She seemed so nice. How could she lock me in the tunnel and try to kill me? I guess you just never know about people.

At least I had a cast of honor on my arm; at school I showed it to everyone. I expected Billy to be proud of me when she heard my story. Maybe she'd give me a kiss without me having to chase her all over the playground to get it. That would be nice! Maybe a story would be written about this Bible mystery – perhaps a movie would even be made of it. Wow, wouldn't that be something? I'd play the leading role of course. Maybe they'd get Clark Gable or Jimmy Stewart to play Father.

Well, it was just too much to think about. Better to play with my knights and forget the past few weeks. One of the gifts I received while in the hospital was one of the knights I had been hoping to get: Sir Germaine. I had needed him for my collection.

One day Mother asked if we wanted to get some fish and chips. Nancy and I said yes.

"That would be great Mother," I said.

So the three of us went to the fish and chips stand and ordered a full order with four large pieces of fish and a whole pile of chips. Mr. Wellington seemed to be in a good humor. I thought it was pretty hard on him to be accused of the murder just because he had served time before.

We paid for our meal and were about to leave when he stopped us with a question.

"By the way, did they find the Bible at Miss Stone's house?" he asked.

"We don't think so; it's still missing," Mother said.

"That's too bad about Miss Stone. I guess she really hated Rev. Holder, but ended up killing someone else by mistake. I guess that Bible is worth a lot; it sure has pretty colors inside," Mr. Wellington said.

I gasped.

"Yes, I'm sure it does," Mother said. "We have to go now. See you next time."

We left the stand without saying a word, but I knew what Mother was thinking because I was thinking the same thing. When we got around the corner from the stand I asked, "What would he know about the inside of a Gutenberg Bible?"

"I don't know, William," Mother replied. "I was thinking the same thing. I didn't think Mr. Wellington was educated enough to have even known what a Gutenberg Bible is let alone know it has colored designs inside."

"But why did he say that?" I persisted.

"I don't know. Let's forget it and get home and have some fish and chips." she said.

I know Mother; when she says let's forget it that means she is concerned. I let it go for the time being. It didn't seem to make sense to me, but this whole thing didn't make sense. We went straight home and ate the fish and chips.

Mother said Nancy and I could sleep in her bed that night. As we were getting ready for bed, we heard a noise downstairs.

"What was that?" I asked.

"It sounded like the front door opening and closing," Nancy said.

"Quickly, hide behind the couch and be very quiet," Mother instructed.

We heard footsteps coming up the stairs very slowly. Certain steps creaked, and we knew where each one was. If it had been Father, he would have slammed the door and yelled that he was home, so it couldn't be him. Mr. Walsh would not come into our apartment without knocking first. Mr. Styles had a key, but he would knock first, too. So who was coming up our stairs?

We could hear the creaking at the fifth step and then again at the eighth step. I could feel Mother trembling beside me.

"Mother," I whispered, "I could get the poker out of the fireplace to use as a weapon."

"Shush," she said.

We stayed very quiet and waited. Whoever it was seemed to be looking in our bedrooms first. Then the footsteps came our way. We were terrified, but couldn't move. Suddenly there stood Mr. Wellington in front of us with a gun in his hand. It was a 45-caliber automatic. I recognized it because Father had one just like it that he used on the Air Force pistol team.

"Well, isn't this cozy? Here we are together at last," Mr. Wellington said.

"What do you want here?" Mother asked.

"Nothing much, Mum. Just to get my property back and put you someplace where no one will ever find you again. If you'll be so kind as to stand and follow me please," he instructed.

"Where are we going?" Mother asked.

"Stop with all the annoying questions, and come with me," Mr. Wellington ordered.

He pointed the gun at us; we had no choice but to follow him. He went downstairs to the old kitchen, got the keys from behind the door and led us into the basement. He knew right where those keys were I thought to myself. He pulled a large flashlight out of his pocket and proceeded to the tunnel door. Since it was broken off its hinges he just motioned for us to go through. Then he went straight for the long tunnel door and opened it. Because of his swift, confident movements I knew he had done this before.

After he opened the door he told us to get in. He made us walk back about 10 feet and then told us to stop. There in the tunnel I could smell that fish smell. It was the same odor I'd smelled before. He set the flashlight down on a rock so it shinned directly at us, and he told us not to move.

"I just need to pick up what belongs to me," he said.

He started pulling rocks out of the wall. They were loose and seemed to come out easily. From behind the rocks he pulled out a large, wrapped bundle. We recognized it immediately as the Gutenberg Bible that we had found.

"That's not your property," I said.

"Be quiet, William," Mother said.

"It's my property now kid, so shut your trap!" Mr. Wellington shouted. "Now if you'll just get down on your knees with your hands up on your head please."

We did as he instructed. I knew what he was about to do, but there was nothing we could do to stop him. Nancy began to cry.

"I hope you don't mind staying down here for a bit love, like the rest of your life. Sorry, but I couldn't let you live with what you know," he explained. "It's nothing personal you see, but I saw the expression on your face when I asked about the Bible today. I guess that was pretty stupid of me, but I'm making up for it now. If you want to say any prayers, now is the time."

"You'll never get away with this," Mother said.

"I am getting away with it, love," he replied.

"Inspector Edwards," I yelled, "you're just in time!"

"I'm not falling for that old trick," Mr. Wellington said.

It wasn't a trick! Inspector Edwards jumped him, and they rolled on the floor of the tunnel. A shot rang out and then another. And then the tunnel began to rumble. Not again! The reverberations from the gun were causing the ceiling to cave in. I put my broken arm up over my head hoping the rocks would hit my cast and not something more vital. I heard Mother scream, and then I blacked out. The next thing I remembered was coughing and trying to get dust and dirt out of my mouth.

"Mother, where are you? Nancy, can anybody hear me?" I yelled.

I listened but all I heard was groaning off in the distance, or at least it seemed that way.

"Is anyone there?" I called again.

Nothing, just some more groaning, but it didn't sound like Mother or Nancy; it sounded like a man.

I hoped I wasn't trapped in the tunnel with Mr. Wellington. Wouldn't that be great?

Just then a familiar voice called to me, "William, is that you?"

"Yes, it's me. Is that you Inspector Edwards?" I asked.

"Yes, my boy, I'm over here. Could you give me a hand? I seem to have my leg caught under some rocks," he said.

I crawled to where I heard his voice, feeling my way through the rubble. I couldn't see a thing and my head was throbbing.

"I'm coming Inspector, I'm coming," I said.

A few more feet and I felt his arm and face.

"Let me try and move some of these rocks off your leg," I said.

"Easy does it, laddie, my leg really hurts. I hope I haven't broken it," Inspector Edwards said.

"I'll be careful. This one is rather large and with my broken arm I don't know if I can move it, but I'll try," I said.

"I'll help you," he replied.

The rock was big, but it was balanced in our favor and rolled off the inspector's leg without falling on him.

"There, that ought to do it. You're leg is free now, Inspector Edwards. Let me feel if there is any broken bone sticking out," I said.

"Careful there my lad, careful," he cautioned.

"I'm being careful. I know what a broken bone feels like, believe me!" I said.

After running my hand down Inspector Edwards' leg and finding no broken bone sticking out, I felt his other leg for the same thing.

"Doesn't seem to be any broken bones, but there is a wet spot here," I said.

"Ouch, careful laddie, that hurts," he said.

"I can't see, but you've got a hole in your pants there and your leg is bleeding," I said.

"I believe you're right, William; I think I've been shot. The question is, what are we going to do now?" he asked.

"Do you have any matches Inspector?" I asked.

"Yes, right here in my vest pocket, why?" he queried.

"Well, I thought if we could find something to burn we could make a torch or something," I said.

"Good thinking my lad," Inspector Edwards replied. "You know, you'd make a fine inspector for Scotland Yard."

"I would, really?" I asked incredulously.

"Yes my lad, you have all the makings of a first-rate detective," he said. "Here's the matches, but what can we burn?"

"How about a piece of your pants? They're ripped anyway," I asked.

I took a torn piece from Inspector Edwards' pants and lit it. There was not much light, but enough for us to see that Mother and Nancy were laying close to us, both with rocks on top of them.

I began to take rocks off Mother while Inspector Edwards held the cloth wrapped around a small, jagged piece of wood so I could see.

"She's still breathing," I said.

"Hurry lad, because this torch isn't going to last much longer," he said.

"Mother, Mother! Are you all right?" I cried.

She didn't answer, but she was breathing hard. I took several rocks off her and then went to check on Nancy.

"I don't see Ted Wellington," Inspector Edwards said.

"Who cares about him, I've got to help Mother and Nancy," I responded.

I crawled over to Nancy; in the dim light I could see her moving and beginning to come around.

"Nancy, are you all right?" I asked.

"William, is that you? Where's Mother? What happened? Are we ...," she jabbered.

"Don't talk, you'll be all right," I interrupted. "Mother is right over here and she's fine. Inspector Edwards is right here with us. We just had a little accident, that's all."

"What happened?" Nancy asked again.

"I guess when the gun went off it caused the tunnel to collapse, but we're all right," I said.

The light went out.

"Help, Mother, William, no please . . . ," she pleaded.

"It's all right Nancy, we just have to get some more cloth to light. How about part of your nightgown?" I asked.

"My nightgown?" Nancy asked.

"Yes, just tear some off the bottom so we can light it and be able to see," I explained.

So Nancy tore the bottom off her nightgown, and Inspector Edwards wrapped it around the old piece of wood he found among the rubble and lit the edge.

"We've got to find something bigger to wrap this cloth around," he said. "I can't hold this small stick without burning my hands."

"Farther down the tunnel there are some timbers that were used to hold up the sides of the tunnel. Maybe we can use one of them for a torch?" I asked.

"How do you know that?" the inspector asked.

"Remember, I was trapped in this tunnel for days, and I feel that I know every part of it," I replied.

"That's right, so you were laddie. Do you think you could spare some more of your nightgown, Nancy, so I could tie it around my leg and stop this bleeding?" Inspector Edwards asked.

Nancy obliged, tearing off some more of her nightgown, and I tied it around Inspector Edwards' leg.

We looked all around, but could not see Mr. Wellington. Either he was buried under the rubble where we couldn't see him or he had escaped the cave-in and was gone.

"How come Mr. Wellington isn't in here with the rest of us?" I asked.

"Well, the last thing I remember before the roof fell in on me," Inspector Edwards said, "was Ted rolling away from me. He could have rolled free of the cave-in or he's buried under there somewhere."

"So we're here in all this mess, Mother's hurt, you're hurt, my head is bleeding and he's out there somewhere free!" Nancy exclaimed.

"Now, now let's not jump to any conclusions; our first order of business is to make sure Mrs. Allen is all right and then see if we can dig our way out of here," Inspector Edwards said.

We spent the rest of the night moving rocks as best we could. Mother awoke and seemed all right, so she began to help. She made a better bandage for Inspector Edwards' leg out of part of her nightgown and then proceeded to find a miracle for us all. Mother found a flashlight laying on the ground. It must have been the one Mr. Wellington was carrying. All we knew was that it was a good one and gave off a lot of light.

Inspector Edwards was relieved that his fingers were not burning anymore. With the new light and some renewed hope, we all began to move rocks, but the job seemed hopeless. There were just too many. From what we could tell, the cave-in must have filled in most of the rooms we had come through to get to this tunnel. Our only hope seemed to be escaping through the tunnel in the other direction, so that's what I suggested.

"But, William," Mother said, "you were trapped way inside that tunnel. Don't you remember your Father had to dig you out and then carry you all the way back here?"

"Yes, I remember, Mother, but I think it's our only chance of getting out of here," I said.

"William, your mother may be right. If you were trapped by a cave-in farther down the tunnel, how could we get through? It would be just like this end." Inspector Edwards said.

"Not really Inspector, you see I was trapped by a cave-in, but they dug me out and that means there is a hole there we could get through and continue to the other end, wherever that is," I replied.

"But William, that is a long shot, as you say in America. What chance do you think we have?" he asked.

"More than we have here. We can't get through this stuff on this end. I propose we try for the other end. How about if we vote on it?" I suggested.

"Whatever you say my boy, whatever you say," Inspector Edwards replied.

So that's exactly what we did; we voted. Mother and Nancy agreed that we were getting no where moving rocks so they voted with me; Inspector Edwards went along to make it unanimous. With our bright flashlight, courtesy of Mr. Wellington, we made our way slowly back through the tunnel where I had spent several nights alone. I didn't mention the rats, figuring that Mother and Nancy would find out soon enough.

We came to the stream and all had a refreshing drink. Mother washed Inspector Edwards' wound and rebandaged it while he took a well-deserved rest. We all needed a rest, and it was getting colder. With Mother and Nancy in nightgowns, what was left of them anyway, and me in pajamas, we were not exactly dressed for this journey. Fortunately, Inspector Edwards was wearing an overcoat; he let Mother and Nancy borrow it. They took turns wearing it to stay warm. I wasn't very cold, and I had things on my mind.

"Inspector, how did you know we were in trouble?" I asked. "I thought you were in London and Miss Stone was the killer."

"That's right William," he said. "I did think Miss Stone was the killer, but after careful investigation I thought otherwise. It turns out that she had received a phone call from her mother Christmas Day at 8:15 in the morning. The call lasted until 8:35 am. This has been verified by telephone company records. Since it was about a 10-minute walk from her home to the church, she would not have gotten there before 8:45 a.m.

"The coroner's report stated that death occurred approximately between 8 and 8:30 that morning," he continued. "He said blood clotting was the key to understanding this. If that was true, she was innocent.

On top of that, we got a call from an agent who worked with the OSS, or Office of Secret Service, during World War II, and he said that Ted Wellington, whose real name is Fredrick Gustauv, was a German double agent. He had been recruited by the German SS, or secret police, and made an assassin. He was also told to infiltrate British intelligence. He got this job because he spoke English very well. One of his cover jobs was as a fish and chips peddler. As soon as I heard that I headed straight here because I knew you might be in danger."

"You were right about that!" Nancy said.

"I guess I got here just in time," the inspector said.

Back at the base Father had been doing some investigating of his own. An Interpol friend told him about Mr. Wellington's background. Interpol is an international police organization that coordinates police activities throughout Europe, except in the communist countries. Father figured that Inspector Edwards knew as well and was already on the case. But Father wasn't taking any chances; he too had headed to Soham as soon as he understood the implications of Mr. Wellington being a free man.

It was after dark when Father reached our home; all the lights were on and the front door was open. He ran upstairs calling to Mother as he went, but there was no reply. He found the bed in front of the large fireplace in the living room where he figured we all were going to sleep together, but no one was there.

He called out but got no answer. Then all of a sudden there was a loud noise, like a train going through the house. He ran downstairs just as Mr. and Mrs. Walsh were coming out of their apartment.

"What was that noise?' Father asked.

"I don't know Master Sergeant Allen; we heard it too," Mr. Walsh replied.

That was the first time Mr. Walsh had used Father's military title.

"It sounded like it came from the basement," Mrs. Walsh said.

"That's just what I thought," Father said.

"I'm going down there," he said.

"I'll be right behind you," Mr. Walsh said. "Just let me get on a coat and grab a flashlight."

Father went back upstairs, found my flashlight, raced to the basement and then to the tunnel. However, he could go no farther than the first door because the rubble from the cave-in blocked the passage.

Father thought he heard someone running down the front hallway but dismissed it as being Mr. Walsh coming down to meet him. What he didn't know and couldn't have known, was that Mr. Wellington had escaped the cave-in and had run out the front door just before Father entered the basement. Mr. Wellington had the Gutenberg Bible in his hands and that was all he cared about.

His escape from the cave-in was miraculous to say the least. When he had heard the rumble in the tunnel and the rocks began to fall from the ceiling he ran as fast as he could and just barely escaped the main crash. He had been hit by a few rocks, but not enough to cause serious injury. By the time anyone figured out that he was missing, he'd be in Europe spending his money. He had contacts in Germany who owed him favors and he was going to collect.

When Father and Mr. Walsh saw the cave-in they couldn't believe their eyes.

"Not a second time," Father said. "Where is my family? Are they trapped in there? Mr. Walsh, get the constable and have him round up every available man. We're going to need all the help we can get to remove all these rocks."

"Yes sir," Mr. Walsh said.

He was off immediately and awoke the whole town in the process. In the meantime Father couldn't figure out what happened to Inspector Edwards, so he called Scotland Yard. They told him he had left on the train for Soham earlier that day and that he should be there by now. With a little checking at the local pub, Father managed to find the cabbie who had brought Inspector Edwards from the train station. The cabbie said he had dropped the inspector off at St. Andrew's about 8 p.m. He said that the inspector was in such a hurry that he didn't give him a tip.

Father left the pub and headed straight for Mr. Wellington's fish stand, but he was not there. In fact, Mr. Wellington appeared to have left the stand without closing up shop. Now Father really believed that Mr. Wellington was the murderer.

As Father returned to St. Andrew's, many questions popped in his mind: What had Mr. Wellington done to his family? Were they all trapped inside the tunnel? Did Mr. Wellington force them all down there, including Inspector Edwards, put them in the tunnel and then blow it up somehow? But how did he get away without being seen? Maybe he didn't get away after all. Maybe he's down there with them?

There were too many questions without answers. The only thing left to do was dig. The local constable showed up with eight men who had volunteered to help. Most had been together playing drafts, or darts as we Americans call it, but they all liked me, or those Yanks, as they referred to my family.

The men dug in to clear away rocks, but they seemed to get nowhere. They dug all through the night, but by dawn everyone was exhausted and they had found nothing. Several of the men returned home to get some sleep, but a couple stayed with Father and the constable to continue digging. They found some shovels and tried to use them, but bare hands with some gloves worked the best.

Father recognized this part of the tunnel as being the large room that led to the long tunnel because the door had been broken off at the entrance.

"We're never going to get through this without some help or large machinery," he said.

"You can't get any tractor down here," the constable replied. "My suggestion is that we get some sleep and tomorrow we come back with more men. I know that's not what you want to hear Master Sergeant Allen, but we have no choice. The men are exhausted and need some rest."

"You're right and I know it, but I just can't help wondering if they're all right," Father replied. "Go home all of you and thank you for what you've done so far. If you can come back tomorrow and bring some help with you, then please do. I need your help. Also, Mr. Wellington, the fish guy, is the cause of all this. He's the murderer of Mr. Cox and the one who stole the Gutenberg Bible. Be on the look out for him in case he's still around."

Everyone said they would be back, fueled by anger at knowing who the murderer was. The word went out throughout Soham to be on the look out for Mr. Wellington even though he was long gone.

After escaping the tunnel collapse, the first thing Mr. Wellington had done was head for his apartment, grab a bag that was already packed with his belongings, pick up his car keys to his old Morris Minor and drive out of town headed for the English Channel. There he could find a ferry to France. His passport was in order so he wouldn't have any trouble getting out of England. The faster he got there the better because Scotland Yard might already have notified the local authorities about him.

On the other hand, maybe he should not be in such a hurry to get out of England. What if they were expecting him to make a dash for the coast? Maybe he should get a new passport with a new name and change his hair color. That's what he'd do. He knew a bloke in London who could do the job for him, but what about money? He'd want quite a sum for a job like this, especially if he had heard through the grapevine about the murder and the missing Bible.

No problem, no problem, Mr. Wellington thought. He would just get the guy to do the job for a small down payment and then when he picked up the passport he'd just have to do away with him. At this point another murder didn't matter.

Mr. Wellington's mind wasn't what you'd call normal. Whatever worked for him was all that mattered to him. If someone got in his way, he'd just dispose of them. Besides, the British were the enemy and he had not forgotten the war. He was not going to get a pension from the Nazis, so this Gutenberg Bible was the answer to his future financial condition.

Firm in his decision, Mr. Wellington pointed his Morris Minor toward London. No one knew he had this car, but they knew what he looked like. He would have to change his appearance and do it in a hurry. He stopped in a small town on the way to London and bought some hair dye. His hair was black and rather long so the first thing to do was cut his hair and change the color.

Mr. Wellington spent the night in a small inn; the next morning he headed for a barber shop and got a haircut. The barber asked a lot of questions, but Mr. Wellington was his usual tight-lipped self. After the haircut he headed for a restroom where he could dye his hair. He made a mess doing it, but managed to clean it up so as not to leave any evidence that he had been there.

Now with short brown hair, Mr. Wellington proceeded to London where he stole some new clothes. He had always looked like a local worker with his old disguise; with his new, short brown hair he decided to take on the guise of a distinguished gentlemen. The clothes were made of the finest material: a herringbone tweed with a waistcoat, or vest, a proper shirt and collar, and a very British tie. He topped it off with a bola hat and full-length coat. When he looked in the mirror, he felt like he was observing a banker on his way to the business district of London.

There was just one thing wrong: the scar running down the left side of his face. How was he going to disguise that? He didn't shave regularly so that his beard kind of covered the scar; now he needed to make it disappear. But how? Maybe a long handlebar moustache; yes, that would do. It would cover most of the scar. But he didn't have time to grow a moustache; he'd have to buy one. This might also arouse suspicion, but the bloke who would do the passport for him would also have other items of interest, like handlebar moustaches.

Following the clothing shoplifting, Mr. Wellington headed straight for his passport friend. The man lived in a third-floor flat, or apartment, in a poor district in London. This, of course, was a front. The man had a secret bank account with enough money in it to choke a horse. Short, fat and jolly, the man greeted Mr. Wellington at the door and ushered him into the parlor.

"Well, well if it isn't my old chum Ted Wellington, or is it some other name you goes by now?" he asked.

"Ted will do fine, but that is going to change with your help," Mr. Wellington replied.

"Oh is it now? Well it's going to cost you some quid my very big newspaper headliner!" the man said.

"How much?" Mr. Wellington asked.

"Well, for a job like this I could get put in the slammer for the rest of my life, so you're going to have to make it worth my while," the man replied.

"How much?" Mr. Wellington asked again.

"I figure 10,000 pounds would do the trick," the man said.

"How much would you have to have now? I don't have that kind of money yet," Mr. Wellington said, laying his trap.

"We'll say 1,000 now and the rest when you pick it up, how's that?" the man asked.

"That'll do fine," Mr. Wellington responded. "Give me a couple of days to come up with the thousand and I'll be back."

They parted company. Mr. Wellington headed for a local bank to open a new account in the name of Francis Dumont. He deposited a small amount and said he would be back to put more in later that week. He told the clerk that he was having a large sum transferred from another bank in Europe, Brussels to be exact. He appeared to be a wealthy man by the looks of him, so the clerk took his application without asking for identification.

What Mr. Wellington was really doing was casing the bank to see how easy it would be to steal a 1,000 pounds. The bank vault appeared to be kept open during business hours so clerks could easily go in and out while tending to their business. Mr. Wellington stayed there long enough to see his opportunity. He asked about opening a checking account for a new business and while he was filling out the paperwork with false information he watched the clerks going back and forth to the vault.

He noticed that the clerk at the end of the counter would go into the vault and leave his station unattended for just a moment. He also noticed that this clerk's station was blocked by a rather large plant sitting next to his window, which blocked the view of the security guard sitting by the front door of the bank. If he waited until the right moment it would be possible to walk up to the hidden station, reach inside the wire and grab enough money to take care of his friend and possibly a lot more, so that's just what Mr. Wellington did.

He managed to get away with more than 2,000 pounds. He simply slipped the money inside his coat pocket and walked casually out of the bank.

Not a bad day's work, if he did say so himself. The bank would notice the money missing by the end of the day, but no one would suspect him.

The next day he took the money to the surprised fat man and asked him how long it would take to get a new passport. With his new moustache and photo, it would only take a few hours to get the passport ready. It would be ready the next day, the fat man told him.

The next day he picked up his new passport, murdered the fat man by breaking his neck, recovered his 1,000 pounds and found another 5,000 in the man's safe. Mission accomplished, Mr. Wellington headed for the coast.

With 7,000 pounds in his pocket, Mr. Wellington could buy a first-class ticket to any destination in Europe. No one was going to stop a respectable-looking businessman on a trip to Paris. Maybe he'd go by plane. But what about the Bible? He couldn't afford to be caught with the Bible at the airport, especially if the police were searching for it, which they most certainly would be. What if he laid low for a while until the heat was off? He had enough money to last some time, so that was a possibility. On the other hand, he wanted to get out of England quickly. He didn't want to stay and face the possibility of getting caught. What was he doing to do?

CHAPTER 8

More Tunnel Troubles

We came to the place in the tunnel where I had been trapped by the cave-in after Father had saved me. There was a space to crawl through right in the middle just like I had thought. The old bricks and stones were hard on Mother's knees, but she made it through OK. I figured that Nancy would gripe and complain, but she didn't – much to my surprise. Inspector Edwards limped badly, but he didn't complain either. We were quite the sight: me with a cast on my arm and in PJs, Mother and Nancy in their torn nightgowns wearing Inspector Edwards' overcoat and him dressed like a banker. Too bad we didn't have a camera to take a picture for the newspaper.

I could just see the headline: Scotland Yard Inspector and Allen Family Lost in Underground Tunnel! It was an interesting thought and indicated how my mind was wandering because of cold and hunger. We'd had some cold water back at the stream, although Mother didn't want to drink it because she thought there might be germs in it. She did wash her face and clean up a little. Both Mother and Nancy had been hit on the head by falling rocks and their heads were cut, but the bleeding had stopped. Nancy did complain of a headache. What else was new? We all had headaches because we were hungry.

During my previous stint in the tunnel I'd gone no farther than this point, so we no longer knew what to expect. We were careful not to make any loud noises – we certainly didn't want to experience any more cave-ins. We began to slow our pace not knowing what was ahead. The ceiling was high enough that only Inspector Edwards had to crouch. He hit his head a few times, and I heard him mumble to himself in aggravation.

We came to a place in the tunnel where it curved to the right, but there were no side tunnels. This was good because we wouldn't have known which way to go if we did come to a fork in the tunnel. From what Mr. Walsh had told us, this tunnel was supposed to go all the way to another town. It had been an escape tunnel long ago for a king. I guess he feared his enemies and had the tunnel built so he could get away in a hurry if necessary.

Just then Nancy screamed, "Rats!"

I knew we'd run into them eventually.

"Don't worry Nancy, just pick up a few rocks and throw them at them when you see them, and they'll run away, believe me I know," I said, staying calm.

"But I hate rats," Nancy squealed.

"It's all right Miss Allen; the light from the flashlight and the noise we make coming through the tunnel will most likely scare them away long before we get to them," Inspector Edwards said.

"That's right honey. Don't be scared, you'll be all right. Just stay close to us," Mother said reassuringly.

"But Mother, I thought you were afraid of rats too," Nancy said.

"I don't care for them any more than you do, but we can't worry about rats; we need to find a way out of this tunnel. If you want to pray for something, pray for that," Mother said.

"How far to you think we've come Inspector?" I asked.

"It's hard to tell Master William, but I believe we've gone at least a mile or two," he replied.

"Mr. Walsh said this tunnel was about three miles long and went to some other town, Ely, I think," I said.

"That could be true William. Ely is about three miles from Soham I believe," Inspector Edwards said.

"So we only have about a mile to go?" I asked.

"Let's hope that's all it is and that we can get out when we get to the other end of this tunnel," Mother said.

"Shhh, quiet everybody. What's that sound?" I asked.

A low rumbling sound was accompanied by vibrations in the tunnel.

"Oh no, not another cave-in!" Nancy cried.

"I don't think so love. It sounds like it's coming from above us somewhere," Inspector Edwards said.

"Maybe it's a car and the tunnel is under a road," I said.

"That could be it laddie; you may have something there," he replied.

"If this tunnel does go to another town it stands to reason it would go under a road somewhere. I just hope it hasn't caved in up ahead."

"Let's try to be a little more positive, Inspector, remember we have children here," Mother reminded.

"Sorry, mum," he replied with chagrin.

"Whose a child? I'm going on 16!" Nancy exclaimed.

"Yes dear, I know, I just think we need to be more positive in our thinking, that's all," Mother said.

I thought about adding my two cents, but decided it was best to keep my mouth shut. Mother was right, we needed to be positive and think of a way to get out of the tunnel. Just then we heard a rumble again; this time it was louder.

Meanwhile, Mr. Wellington had figured out what he would do. He'd head for the train station, get a locker and put the Bible in it. Then he'd go straight to the airport and get a first-class ticket for Paris, where he would find a potential buyer. He would figure out how to get the Bible out of England once he had a buyer.

He needed to leave London quickly, before the police found the fat man's body. His whole flat was full of passports, photo equipment and forging materials. Scotland Yard was bound to make the connection and realize Mr. Wellington had disguised himself; officers would be looking for anyone of his general height and description.

Mr. Wellington took a cab to the Marble Arch Station and put the Gutenberg Bible in a locker. No one would know it was there except him, and no one seemed to pay attention when he put the package in the locker. It was locker No. 714. He had to remember that – but why worry? It was on the key. He just couldn't lose the key. His next stop was Heathrow Airport, where he purchased a first-class ticket to Paris. He used cash to get the ticket, but no one seemed to care. He appeared to be the businessman he told the customs agent he was. He even had a businessman's briefcase. He kept some cash on him, but put the rest in his check-in luggage. He knew he was taking a chance doing that – but it was stolen money after all. If someone stole it from him, he could simply steal more.

The airport was busy, which worked in his favor. He boarded the plane after eating lunch. The plane was full except for first class. There seemed to be just him and an old lady who was traveling to France to see her granddaughter. She told everybody she saw her reason for traveling. It wasn't long before she spotted Mr. Wellington and drew him into a long conversation, mostly one-sided, about her granddaughter, her family and her dog.

Back at the tunnel, a few rocks fell from the ceiling, but no cave-in, thank God. The rumble had stopped for now, but we didn't know how much more the tunnel could take. We had to move faster.

"I know your leg hurts, Inspector, but we really need to pick up the pace and get to the end of this tunnel before the whole thing falls in on us," Mother said.

"I thought we were going to be more positive, Mother," I reminded.

"Yes, you're right, William. I'm positive we need to move faster and get out of here," Mother retorted.

"Faster it is, mum. Let me take the lead and shine the light up ahead just in case," Inspector Williams said.

"Lead the way," she replied.

With Inspector Edwards up front, I felt a little better. I had been in the lead with the light, but it was really his place. I think he was just trying to make me feel good, or like a man, by letting me lead. We could hear the rats scurrying up ahead of us. Every once in a while one of them stayed back, and we almost stepped on it. Nancy had a fit, but she was getting braver as we went. I was proud of her because she had always cried or threw a fit if things didn't go her way, but she was different down here in the tunnel. I think she was so scared she didn't know how to behave.

We had our disagreements, but most of the time we got along as good as any brother and sister would who were six years apart. I liked to tease her, especially when she had a boyfriend come over. I would hide behind the couch while they were alone. Just at the right time, when they were about to kiss, I'd jump out and yell "Boo!" and then run down the hall. Nancy would get so mad she would chase me all over the house, but I'd run to Mother and tell her Nancy was being mean to me and that would be that. I suppose that I was being a rat, but it was fun.

It looked like we were going to spend the night in the tunnel. It was cold and damp and generally unpleasant. Mother, Nancy and I huddled under the inspector's overcoat while he braved the cold. He said that he was all right, but I knew he must be uncomfortable with his leg shot. He didn't complain, though. We spent the night in the dark listening to an occasional rumble above us. We figured that we were under a road and that cars were crossing overhead, but it still made us nervous because we didn't know if the roof would cave in or not. This wasn't conducive to sleeping, but we must have dozed off because when I woke up Inspector

Edwards was tugging on my arm. His voice sounded like it was a long way off.

"William, William, it's time we got moving. Can you hear me?" he said.

"Yes Inspector, I hear you, I'm awake. I'll get Mother and Nancy up," I replied.

We were all stiff and cold and hungry. Trying to move was difficult. My muscles were sore and my broken arm ached. Inspector Edwards tried his best to cheer us up, talking about getting out of the tunnel and how he was going to treat us all to a nice dinner, but I knew he was hurting himself and was just trying to make us feel better. He was a brave man – maybe not as brave as Father – but still a brave man.

The flashlight was working well after leaving it off all night to save the batteries. We started out once again, heading for the end of the tunnel, wherever that was! The tunnel had been curving to the right, but now it seemed we were going straight again. It's funny, but we didn't hear any rats all night and hadn't seen any since waking.

"Everyone stop for a minute," Inspector Edwards commanded.

"What is it?" Mother asked.

"Just be quiet for just a minute, mum; I think I heard something," he answered.

We stood very quiet and listened, for what we didn't know. Then we heard it, the sound of water rushing. It sounded kind of like a waterfall up ahead someplace.

"That's water coming from up ahead somewhere," Inspector Edwards said.

"It's on my feet," Nancy yelled.

Sure enough, the water was coming from someplace and began rushing past our feet. It was cold and now our slippers were soaked.

"Maybe there is a hole up ahead somewhere, and it's raining outside," Mother suggested.

"That could be, mum, that could be," the inspector replied.

"But it seems to be rising," I pointed out.

"You don't suppose a water main broke do you?" Mother asked.

"I don't know Mrs. Allen, but we've got to keep going in this direction; we can't go back," Inspector Edwards said seriously.

So we continued to slosh through the water that was now ankle deep and very cold. The rats showed up trying to escape the water only they were escaping in our direction. Fortunately, they went by fast, but every once in a while we'd step on one, and it would let out with a squeal.

We needed to find the end of the tunnel quickly because we were all getting tired. The cold water and damp tunnel wasn't doing our health any good. The water wasn't getting any deeper; in fact, it seemed to be getting lower. Maybe it was a rainstorm like Mother had thought, and it had ended. I don't know, but we were thankful. Now the floor of the tunnel was just muddy.

"What's this here?" Inspector Edwards queried.

He shined his light on what appeared to be two skeletons on the floor of the tunnel. They were very old, perhaps hundreds of years old. Each one had on armor and a chain vest. Inspector Edwards said this was called chain mail and knights wore it to protect themselves during battle. The men were laying down with a sword in one hand and a shield in the other. One man had a dagger sticking out of his rib cage and both swords looked rusty like they had dried blood on them.

"Evidently these poor chaps killed each other in some sort of fight, and it appears from what they are wearing that this fight took place a long time ago," the inspector said.

"One shield has three red lions on it," I noticed. "Do you know what that means Inspector Edwards?"

"I'm not sure, laddie, but usually red lions meant royalty of some sort. See, he also has red lions across his chain mail as well," he said.

"The other guy has yellow and black stripes on his shield," I said. "What does that mean?"

"I don't know, William, but we can find out later when we get out of this terrible place. There is a book called the *Book of Heraldry,* which will have the answers to the questions we're asking," came the inspector's answer.

We carefully stepped over the remains of the knights and continued on our way. Mother and Nancy didn't have much to say about the discovery except some ughs and oohs. The tunnel was still wet, but at least there were no cave-ins and the way was clear up ahead.

"Look!" Nancy yelled.

"What is it?" Mother asked.

"Turn off your flashlight Inspector Edwards and look up ahead," Nancy instructed.

With the light off, we could see it. There was a light up ahead, though it looked like it was a long way off.

"What do you suppose it is?" Nancy question.

"I don't know, love, but we're going to find out. Come on let's get going," Inspector Edwards said.

With renewed pep in our step, we turned the flashlight back on and headed for the light. As we got closer to it, the light got brighter and we thought we heard music.

"Do you hear that? It sounds like music," I said.

Sure enough, it was music. It sounded like a radio program. As we got closer, we could hear it more clearly. It was some sort of British comedy program. We heard someone announce the name Willford Pickles.

"I know him," the inspector said. "He's a comedian here in England."

We got to the end of the tunnel and could see the light plainly now. It was coming from around the edges of the door that was at the end tunnel. Of course it was locked, but we could see light coming from the other side, and we could still hear Mr. Pickles on the radio.

"Let's yell," Mother suggested. "Maybe someone will hear us."

So we all began yelling at the top of our lungs. Inspector Edwards also began pounding on the door with the flashlight.

"Stop, I think I hear voices," Inspector Edwards said.

Sure enough, we could hear voices.

"Listen, what are they saying?" Nancy asked.

We strained to hear – someone was saying that they heard yelling coming from behind the wall.

"Yes, it's us, and we're trapped here in this tunnel! Get help, and get us out of here," Mother yelled.

Whoever was on the other side of the wall turned off the radio and called back to us: "We hear you, and we're getting help."

The tunnel, it seemed, ended inside someone's home. We wondered who it was and where we were.

Father and the men of Soham had given up on digging us out of the tunnel from the St. Andrew's side and were on their way to Ely where the tunnel was supposed to end. The constable from Soham contacted the Ely constable, and they met with Father at the local police station. The local cops, or bobbies, as they call them in England knew where the old tunnel was and took them straight to an old house near the end of town.

As they arrived and old man burst from the house, running to his car. He stopped when he saw the police and Father and ran to them instead.

"There is someone yelling from behind our wall. I was just on the way to your station to tell you," the old man explained.

"What kind of yelling?" Father asked.

"Well, my missus and I were listening to our favorite radio program when we heard this yelling coming from behind the wall. We turned off the radio and heard it again. There is someone trapped in there I think!" the old man exclaimed.

"Yes, and I think it's my family," Father said.

"What's your family doing trapped behind my wall?" the old man asked.

"It's a long story; I'll be happy to share it with you later, but right now we've got to get them out of there," Father replied.

With the help of some local men, Father broke down the wall inside of the old man's house and then proceeded to break down the door to the tunnel.

We were never so glad to see Father in all our lives. The police had an ambulance at the ready. They took Inspector Edwards to the hospital right away to treat his leg. Mother, Nancy and I were given hot chocolate and blankets to warm us. Father hugged us all; he was relieved and glad we were alive. He told us that there had been no sign of Mr. Wellington. He either got away, which the police and Father suspected, or was buried under the rubble back in Soham. They would find out soon enough when the rubble was cleared away, but that would take awhile because it all had to be done by hand.

We told him how Mr. Wellington had taken us at gunpoint into the tunnel to kill us when Inspector Edwards showed up just in the nick of time. Father said it was fortunate that Inspector Edwards had gotten the information he needed while in London. We told him he had gotten a tip from someone in Europe, but we didn't know who. Father had no comment other than to say that he was just glad that we were alive.

We visited Inspector Edwards in the hospital two days later. The doctor kept him in Ely to keep an eye on him. It seems he came down with pneumonia from being in the tunnel. It's a wonder we weren't sick, but we only had a few sniffles. The inspector promised us that we had a dinner coming as soon as he was out of the hospital. He said he knew of a nice restaurant in London that was famous for its quaint atmosphere and delicious food. We said that would be great and we were looking forward to it. We all needed rest after our ordeal and Nancy and I had to get back to school. I didn't really miss school, but I did miss Billy.

Meanwhile, the trip to Paris was short for Mr. Wellington; he awoke from a deep sleep with the stewardess poking him in the arm and saying that they are arrived. He quickly retrieved his belongings and headed for the door. He smiled and thanked the stewardess on the way out. It was raining in Paris, and he got rather wet walking from the plane to the terminal. He went through customs without any problems and went directly to the cab stations. He took a cab to the Hotel de Ville, where he had a reservation.

The Hotel de Ville is an old and famous Paris landmark. It had been renovated, but since most tourists prefer newer, more modern accommodations it wasn't a hot spot. Mr. Wellington wanted someplace where he could disappear, or at least not be noticed. This was the perfect spot. He had known of this hotel when he was in Paris during the war, but had never stayed as a guest.

He had not been in Paris since the war. Not much had changed except the traffic was worse. The cab passed under the Arc de Triomphe and down the city's most famous boulevard, the Champs-Elysees. Once Mr. Wellington checked into his room he took a shower and ordered some coffee from room service. He would have dinner later when he made contact with the man he had come to Paris to see. This was the only man he knew who could fence something as valuable as a Gutenberg Bible.

Mr. Wellington only knew the man as Pierre, no last name, but he knew where to find him. Pierre had been his contact all through World War II. Mr. Wellington had brought Pierre many treasures stolen from wealthy Jews during the war. He accumulated quite a sum during the war, but then lost most of it trying to transfer it to Switzerland. If that American agent hadn't gotten in his way and tried to expose him, he would have gotten away with millions.

Mr. Wellington had not forgotten this and vowed one day to get back at this man – once he found out who he was. He could not afford to be exposed as a double agent at any cost. He was tired of selling fish and chips. It was time to be rich, take on a new identity and disappear someplace warm. Mr. Wellington was fed up with damp and dreary England. He had friends in Argentina. Yes, maybe that would be where he'd go. He still had some family in Germany, but they didn't care about him and Germany was not a good place to be, at least not for a double agent. That's what everyone believed him to be, but he really was German, or Nazi, through and through.

He had wanted to be in the SS during the war, but that didn't happen. His family did not have the right connections with Heimlich Himmler, who headed the SS and ran Germany's concentration camps. Before and during the war politics had a huge effect on the futures of Germany's elite families. If you were in the right place, or from the right family, at the right time, you could write your own ticket within the Nazi high command. This was not the case for Ted Wellington, a.k.a. Fredrick Gustauv. He wasn't even an important agent, just one of the many who tried to serve Adolf Hitler. That was all behind him now; he wanted to settle down in a place where the people didn't know or care who he was.

If it wasn't for that American brat he'd have been long gone – the Bible would already be sold, and he'd be on his way to a sunny spot. How that Scotland Yard inspector found out who he was mystified Mr. Wellington. He was lucky that he wasn't buried in that tunnel with the rest of them. Wouldn't that have been fun! As much as he wanted revenge on William, selling the Bible and disappearing was more important. He would make the call and meet Pierre later that night.

CHAPTER 9
The Little Black Book

When Inspector Edwards got out of the hospital he returned to London to see if there were any leads on Mr. Wellington. He not only wanted to catch him for stealing the Bible and killing Mr. Cox, but now for the attempted murder of Mother, Nancy and me, not to mention for shooting him. He would limp forever because of Mr. Wellington, and he was determined to find him no matter where he was. His first job was to find out who the Interpol contact was and how he had gotten his information.

After the usual congratulations from his peers in Scotland Yard for still being alive, he made his way to the superintendent's office. What he found out was surprising. The call had come from Interpol, but Interpol would not disclose who made the call. He was told it was a security matter and to let it go at that. But if that person knew about Mr. Wellington and his previous war crimes, maybe he or she would be willing to help find him. It was worth a try.

Inspector Edwards was given complete control of the Gutenberg Bible case. That allowed him greater amounts of money and men for the investigation. He immediately put several men to work finding Mr. Wellington. An artist drew several renditions of Mr. Wellington in different disguises; these were passed out to train station agents, the airline ticket agents and at the docks. Every road in and out of London was spot checked. Cars and trucks carrying anyone close to his description were stopped. Cabs and buses were alerted and a general alarm was out for the man.

The newspapers ran several stories and many pictures of my family with full detail about our ordeal in the tunnel. Mother, Nancy and I had our pictures on the front pages of most British newspapers and tabloids. Inspector Edwards noticed that Father's picture was absent from these articles, which he thought rather strange. He didn't dwell on it though – Master Sergeant Allen was busy with Air Force matters and probably wasn't around when the photos were taken.

Most of the tips Inspector Edwards' task force received were dead ends. No one had seen anyone who matched Mr. Wellington's description traveling with a package that could be the famous Bible. Inspector Edwards was growing frustrated when a lead appeared out of nowhere. Gordon Harvard, a.k.a. the fat man, had been found dead in his London flat. The cause of death, according to the coroner, was a broken neck. It appeared to be a robbery that went wrong. His safe was open and cash was missing.

Once Inspector Edwards had thoroughly searched Mr. Harvard's flat it was obvious that the man forged passports. He found several blank passports from many countries, photographic equipment, disguise kits and all of the goodies needed to make fake passports. There were no fingerprints in the flat except those belonging to Mr. Harvard. The landlady said Mr. Harvard had visitors at all hours of the night, but she never saw anyone up close. This could be because she didn't really see anyone, or didn't want to see anyone. Whatever the case, she didn't provide much information. She said Mr. Harvard paid his rent on time and that was all she cared about.

The search of the flat yielded one lead; Inspector Edwards took it with him. He found a book hidden behind Mr. Harvard's bed that had many names in it. He would start searching for the people in the book and see what transpired. His instructions to the task force? Find everyone listed in the book if possible and question them about their relationship with Mr. Harvard and find out whether they knew Mr. Wellington. Anything out of the ordinary was to be reported to the inspector at once.

The task force members went to work immediately, rounding up the people whose names were in Mr. Harvard's little black book. Most of the people were local and knew nothing about the fat man's work, or so they said. They told the Scotland Yard inspectors that Mr. Harvard had their name by mistake or that he was just a casual acquaintance. If any of them knew anything they weren't saying.

Inspector Edwards was becoming impatient with the lack of progress when one of his men found something. A man listed in the book had a grudge against Mr. Harvard. His name was Oscar Collinsworth. Mr. Harvard was supposed to do a job for Mr. Collinsworth, but he wanted more money than Mr. Collinsworth could pay. Mr. Collinsworth tried to get him to take payments, but Mr. Collinsworth insisted on cash only for the full amount or no deal.

Mr. Collinsworth admitted to the Scotland Yard inspector that he was trying to get a fake passport for his daughter, who was behind the Iron Curtain in East Berlin. When Mr. Harvard reneged on the deal, Mr. Collinsworth was angry and threatened to kill the fat man. This happened two days before Mr. Harvard was found dead.

Mr. Collinsworth said he was glad that Mr. Harvard was dead and wished that he had done it, but he didn't and had a secure alibi. He was out of town at the time Mr. Harvard was killed and could prove it. He and his wife were on holiday, as the British call it, down by Dover on the coast.

It seemed another dead end until Mr. Collinsworth mentioned that when he last saw Mr. Harvard the fat man was in the middle of a big job that would keep him in tea for a few years, as Mr. Collinsworth put it. Mr. Harvard told Mr. Collinsworth that he was busy with another client who needed a rush job and was willing to pay big bucks. He said this man needed to get out of England fast and that he needed a disguise as well as a new passport.

This was the tip Inspector Edwards needed. It created the possibility of a connection between Mr. Wellington and Mr. Harvard. Mr.

Wellington needed a disguise and also needed to get out of England in a hurry. Inspector Edwards called the coroner and asked him to look for anything that could connect Mr. Wellington with the murder of Mr. Harvard. He asked him to check carefully under the fat man's fingernails in case there was some skin or hair that might be Mr. Wellington's. He had a sample of Mr. Wellington's hair from their fight in the tunnel – the inspector had grabbed the man's hair and came away with a handful of it. He had it in his pocket right after the fight.

If the coroner could find someone else's hair on the fat man's body, or possibly in his flat, and if it matched Mr. Wellington's hair, then the inspector had another murder charge against him. And if Mr. Wellington really did flee to another country he would be considered a criminal by Interpol and could be arrested and sent back to England – if anyone could find him. Inspector Edwards realized that Mr. Wellington was probably out of the country and most likely in Europe, but where?

Father had a habit of disappearing for weeks at a time on Air Force business. It was no different in England. Being a senior master sergeant may have had its privileges, but my family never knew where he was or where he had been. He always said the same thing: It was Air Force business and classified. Mother never questioned it, but I always wondered what he was doing when he was gone. If we asked him where he had been, he usually made up an answer, saying it was just an exercise or practice for some type of war game. Once he said he was just flying around for several days checking on weather in a certain area, which I found really strange.

What I didn't know about Father, and wouldn't know for many years, was that he worked for the Office of Secret Service, or OSS. That was his assignment throughout World War II, but we didn't know that. He had to sign an agreement not to say anything to his family in order to protect us from reprisals by people who did not like Father. If they found out who his real family was we could be in danger. Not that we weren't in enough trouble as it was, but there was no sense in making it worse.

In the aftermath of our rescue from the tunnel, Father was on a mission of his own – to find the man who tried to kill his family. We didn't know what he was doing, and neither did Scotland Yard because Father was careful. He had contacts in Europe and other places – men who could find out things that the police couldn't. Their methods were not the same as the police either, but that's why they could get information more easily; they didn't obey the rules that the police had to obey.

One of these men worked out of Interpol's Paris headquarters. Father met this man in Paris in a little café by the River Seine. The word on the streets of Paris was that a man fitting the description of Mr. Wellington was in town looking for someone to fence a rare Gutenberg Bible. There would be a reward for anyone who could lead the police to Mr. Wellington.

Father told his contact that if this information was spread around Paris, every crook in the city would be after Mr. Wellington for the reward alone, which was rumored to be 100,000 francs. Father and his friend spread this rumor and Father, at least, had the money to back it up. Where he got it from, I couldn't say, but he had the money, there was no doubt about that.

Inspector Edwards was a man of his word. He called Mother and invited us to dinner in London. We accepted, of course, but Mother said Father wasn't available because he was out of town on Air Force business. Inspector Edwards asked us to come anyway and Mother accepted, to my surprise.

Two days later we were having dinner in London in the best restaurant I'd ever eaten in. It was called the Elizabethan Room. It was different than any restaurant I had ever been. All the employees were dressed Elizabethan period costumes – the 15th century, Inspector Edwards said. The dining room was huge with high ceilings. The walls were covered with old shields, war clubs, swords, and armor of all shapes and sizes. There was sawdust on the floor because when you finished eating a piece of meat you were expected to throw the remains over your shoulder onto the floor. Dogs grabbed the bones and chewed on them while you were eating.

Inspector Edwards told Mother that children younger than 18 were not permitted in the restaurant, but he got the owner to make a special exception since we were celebrities.

The food the restaurant served was amazing. We started with kangaroo tail soup followed by boar's head and peacock dressed like they hadn't been cooked, but of course they were. They brought the food out on platters that were bigger than me. The waitresses threw rolls at the diners; we were supposed to catch them. All the plates were made of metal and the cups, too. The table must have been longer than 30 feet around which sat 50 or 60 diners. The band that provided dinner music played instruments I'd never seen before. Mother said they were old instruments used during Elizabethan times.

During dinner I explained to Inspector Edwards my theories concerning Mr. Wellington. I told him that if I were him I would change my appearance, hide the Bible somewhere in London and get out of the country as fast as possible with a new identity.

"William, my lad, you are a remarkable young man," he said over dessert. "What you just told me is exactly what we think he's done."

"Really?" I asked.

"Yes, that's right, and what's more is that we feel that he did get out of the country wearing some new disguise with a new passport before we got our people ready to catch him. What we don't know is what he did with the Bible," Inspector Edwards said with some regret in his voice.

"I think I know," I said.

"You do! Well let's have it, lad. What do you think he did with it?" Inspector Edwards asked.

"Well, if I were Mr. Wellington and had to get rid of a very rare Bible but didn't want anyone to know where I put it, I'd put it right in plain sight of everyone," I said.

"Hold on there, laddie; that doesn't make any sense," he replied.

"What I mean is, if I were Mr. Wellington I'd hide the Bible someplace out in the open where lots of people go, but don't pay attention to anyone, like a train station," I explained.

"You mean in a locker in the train station?" he inquired.

"Sure, why not? It's a very busy place and someone could hide a large package like the Bible in a locker and no one would give it another thought, especially if the person hiding the package was not suspicious looking," I said.

"So you think Mr. Wellington, in his new disguise, put the Bible in a locker in a train station here in London someplace, took the key with him and skipped over to Europe where he could contact someone willing to pay the large price needed to get their hands on one of the rarest books in the world? Is that what you think?" Inspector Edwards asked.

"Yes, that's what I think, and I also feel that he had to do it that way because he had to get out of the country in a hurry after killing this guy you said made him a new passport," I added.

"You mean the fat man, Gordon Harvard?" he asked.

"Yeah, him; the guy you told us about earlier this evening. And there's more, too," I went on. "I think if I were this guy who was going to buy the Bible from Mr. Wellington, I would want to see it first or I wouldn't give him a cent. If I'm going to trade some marbles or comic books, I have to see the merchandise first or there's no deal. So Mr. Wellington has to come back to London, pick up the Bible and take it back to Europe if he's going to sell it. But he's going to have to wait until some of the heat is off first. Do you get it Inspector?"

"I think you've been reading too many of those mystery comic books William!" Inspector Edwards laughed. "However, you do have a point about him coming back to get the Bible. He'd have to do that in order to get it over to Europe to sell it; that part I agree with you on."

"It's nice to know you accept my theory, Inspector," I said. "Now, are you going to eat those strawberries, or can I have them?"

Mother caught that last part of our conversation and made a comment about my manners.

"Yes, Mama," I said. I called her mama when I was aggravated at her for getting on to me in front of someone I respected. Inspector Edwards saved me though.

"Mrs. Allen, you know you have a very bright boy here. I believe he'd make a first-rate Scotland Yard inspector," he said.

"You may be right, Inspector, but right now this boy is headed for bed. I want to thank you for the lovely, and very unusual, dinner but we must be going if we are to catch the train at Marble Arch Station," she said.

"My pleasure as always. May I accompany you to the station? I have a car outside, and we can be there in a few minutes," he said.

"Yes, I will except your offer Inspector because it is so late, and I'm not used to being in London at this hour," Mother replied.

So we got to ride in a special Scotland Yard police car. It was much like the cabs with two seats that folded down behind the front seat. Nancy and I sat there while Inspector Edwards and Mother sat across from us. When we got to Marble Arch Station Inspector Edwards came in with us to make sure we got on the train that would take us to our connection up north to Soham. Actually the train didn't go directly to Soham, but it was close enough that we could catch a cab the rest of the way.

When we got into the station I pointed out the key lockers to the inspector; they were in the open areas where people walked by to get to the train level.

"He could have hidden the Bible in a locker just like one of these here," I said.

"That he could, laddie; that he could. As soon as I get back to my office, I'm going to have my task force watch all the lockers at every train station in London," he said.

"Won't that take a lot of men?" I asked.

"Yes, it will, but it has to be done or we'll never find him. If we can catch him taking the Bible out of a locker, we'll have him for sure," the inspector replied.

"But what if he doesn't take the Bible out of the locker himself, but has someone else do it?" I asked.

"What are you saying, William?" Inspector Edwards questioned.

"What I'm saying is if I were going to get this Bible out of the locker without being seen, I'd get someone else to do it," I explained.

"How?" he asked.

"Well, I'd just pay someone to get it out of the locker, telling him that it's my business papers or something like that, and I don't have time to do it. Maybe something like that," I said.

"You amaze me, William, you really do. How do you come up with ideas like this?" Inspector Edwards inquired.

"I don't know, I guess it's my awesome heritage!" I said.

"By the way, William, I forgot to tell you something. You remember those knights we found in the tunnel? Well it turned out that those were two famous knights who hated each other and had challenged each other to a joust, or a duel, but they were never seen or heard of again. They just disappeared according to history," he said.

"How did you find all this out Inspector?" I asked.

"Well, I had the remains taken to the Natural History Museum and the experts there told me all this information," he explained. "It seems that one of the knights, the one with the three red lions on his shield, was a prince in line to be king. The other knight didn't want him to be king, probably because of a woman or something, and so they fought. I guess the fight took them down in the tunnel somehow and that's where it ended with them killing each other."

"Wow, what a story that would be. I wish I could have been there to see that fight," I exclaimed.

"No more stories for now young man. It's time we caught our train and headed home," Mother said.

"Just so you know, Mrs. Allen, the museum is offering a 10,000 pound reward for finding the two knights, and you're going to get it," the inspector said.

"What?" Mother exclaimed.

"That's right, and I'm so sorry for not telling you earlier. I was so excited about dinner and talking to William about the case that it completely slipped my mind. I'll send the paperwork for you in the mail," he said.

"What paperwork?" Mother questioned.

"Oh, it's just some form the museum wants you to fill out telling how you found the knights and all that rubbish!" the inspector said. "Here's you train now, cheerio!"

All the way home I thought about those knights fighting in the tunnel. It must have been some fight. Swords flashing, shields banging together, the men yelling – oh, it must have been something to see. I must have fallen asleep because the next thing I remember was Mother pulling on my sleeve and telling me to get up. We got off the train, caught a cab to Soham and went straight to bed. I dreamt of brave knights killing dragons while riding on gallant horses all decked out in armor and beautiful colors.

I was one of the knights, of course, the bravest of them all. My colors were purple and black. My shield had a cross on it with gold edges. My armor was also black, and I wore a purple cape that flowed out behind me as I rode along. My horse was garbed in purple and black with a silver hood on its head with a large horn sticking out of it. My sword was made of the finest metal, hand forged for hundreds of hours by the king's own blacksmith. What a sight I was riding through Sherwood Forest on the way to my castle.

Far away from the forest and back to the streets of Paris, Mr. Wellington was on his way to meet Pierre. They were supposed to rendezvous at a small café on the West Bank near the Louvre, Paris' most famous art museum. Mr. Wellington was nervous, but he tried not to show it. He had reached the meeting place well ahead of time, scanned the area, but saw no cause for alarm. Pierre showed up right on time. He had gotten fatter since Mr. Wellington had seen him last, and his hair was thinner, too, but he'd never forget that face.

"Well, we meet again Pierre," Mr. Wellington said.

"Nice to see you, too, Fredrick," Pierre said.

"I don't use that name anymore. My name is Francis Dumont," Mr. Wellington replied.

"Francis it is, my friend, but what happened to Ted or whatever your name was in England?" Pierre asked.

"Ted is dead. and I don't want him resurrected," Mr. Wellington said.

"Fine with me," Pierre responded. "Now let's order some coffee or someone will get suspicious about our little meeting."

The coffee was brought by the waiter who looked at each man carefully. He then returned to the kitchen and picked up the phone.

"Now let's get down to business," Pierre said. "Do you have the Gutenberg Bible or not?"

"Yes, I have it, but not here of course. I'm no fool you know," Mr. Wellington said.

"Well I have to see it and have an expert inspect it before I can make you an offer," Pierre replied.

"But I told you I have it and that it is a Gutenberg Bible; what else do you have to know?" Mr. Wellington asked.

"I'm not in the practice of purchasing something without verifying its worth!" Pierre exclaimed.

"How about a down payment to keep me from selling it to someone else?" Mr. Wellington asked.

"First of all, you don't know that many people here. Finding someone else to buy a well-publicized missing Gutenberg Bible would not be a smart move for you; one could assume it would not be in the best interest of your health. Secondly, I happen to know that you have plenty of money and don't need any right now," Pierre countered.

"How could you know that?" Mr. Wellington asked.

"I have my sources. I happen to know that you are wanted for the murder of the fat man in London, and Scotland Yard would probably like to know who robbed one of London's banks the other day," Pierre said.

"You're bluffing," Mr. Wellington said.

"Am I? The news on the street, Francis, or whatever your name is, says your worth 100,000 francs dead or alive," Pierre continued.

"What are you talking about?" Mr. Wellington demanded.

"I'm giving you a chance to get the Bible for me is what I'm talking about. I can get you a lot of money, enough for you to retire for the rest of your life, if you get me that Bible. But if you can't do it, then your life is not worth much as it stands right now," Pierre said. "I can get you to a safe house and protect you for a while, but I have to have the Bible first."

"But if I go back to England so soon, I could get caught!" Mr. Wellington exclaimed.

"So the Bible is still in England is it? What a fool you are. Why didn't you bring it with you?" Pierre asked.

"How could I do that? It would have been discovered at customs," Mr. Wellington said.

"That's your problem," Pierre responded. "You get the Bible so I can have it inspected or you get nothing. It's your choice."

Mr. Wellington parted company with Pierre just as two men came into the café. They asked the waiter about the two men and then they left.

I didn't know it at the time, but Father was also in Paris looking for Mr. Wellington. He had Interpol agents looking for him, too. There were just too many places in Paris for someone to hide. It never occurred to them that Mr. Wellington would stay in a plush hotel like the Hotel de Ville. He had a better disguise than they thought. The waiter at the café had described the two men: one was very short and fat with thin hair, and the other was wearing a dark overcoat and French beret over his face so that it was hard to see what he looked like. The handlebar moustache showed, though. Mr. Wellington had been smart. He didn't show up at a French café in the middle of the night wearing a business suit. That would have been a dead giveaway. He disguised himself to look like a local.

Mr. Wellington returned to his hotel without incident, but now he was scared. What if it was true that he was wanted on the street dead or alive? Every crook in Paris would be looking for him. He was going to have to return to London quickly, get the Bible out of the locker and get it to Paris, but how?

No matter, he was smart and he'd figure something out on the way back. Scotland Yard probably wouldn't expect him to return to England so quickly. In fact, the inspectors probably thought he was still in London. Or did they? It didn't matter. What did matter was that he was going back and quickly.

He called the airport and made a reservation for London for the next day. He would have to take a chance. If he was going to get the money for that Bible and head for Argentina, he'd have to do it now. Mr. Wellington was a man of action. He had made it through the war without getting caught; this would be no different than any other mission except that this time he was doing it for himself, not someone else.

The next day Mr. Wellington checked out of his hotel and headed for the airport. His flight was on time, and he got to London just at teatime – when all of England takes a break and enjoys tea. He decided to take a chance and head straight for the Marble Arch Station and retrieve the Bible. He had decided on the plane that he would not get the Bible out of the locker himself, but pay someone else to do it.

As he entered the station, he saw a boy of about 15 years old waiting for a train. He told the boy that if he got a package out of locker 714 with no questions asked, he'd give him five pounds. The boy agreed and did just that. He went to the locker, put in the key, took out the package and headed straight for the restroom where Mr. Wellington had told him to meet him. He got his five pounds and went on his way. Mr. Wellington had purchased a large suitcase to put the Bible in, which he did before he left the restroom. He was just another businessman stopping in the restroom to freshen up a bit before catching his train.

Like everyone else, the Scotland Yard men watching the lockers at Marble Arch Station were taking their tea. With their guard down they never saw the boy take the package from the locker, nor did they notice Mr. Wellington walking through the train station, headed for the cab stand. He caught a cab and went directly to Palace Hotel, where he had booked a room.

Mr. Wellington was relieved to have made it this far without being spotted. Now for the next part of his plan. He decided that taking the plane back to Paris would be no good. For one reason, it was too soon for Francis Dumont to return, and there was the question of how to get the Bible through customs.

Mr. Wellington thought there was a better way. He'd go by boat so he could keep an eye on the Bible. His plan was to ship the Bible as a package marked ash trays to the Hotel de Ville in Paris. No customs officer would suspect anything but ash trays in the box, not on a boat with too many other boxes to check. French customs officers were not that particular. He was sure it would get through. This time he would be on holiday. This time he would be just another fisherman going to Europe on a boat to find the perfect fish in French rivers. That was his plan.

Mr. Wellington went to a London sporting goods store, purchased a rod and reel, a tackle box, some waders and other fishing gear. He then took a cab for the Dover coast where he would catch a boat to France. He stopped along the way to mail his package of ash trays addressed to the Hotel de Ville in Paris. He knew he'd get there before the package arrived and be able to intercept it without any problem. If he didn't get there in time, then someone at the hotel would be rich. But that wasn't going to happen; Mr. Wellington would make sure of that.

Inspector Edwards was not in a good mood. So far not one of his agents had reported anything suspicious or noteworthy. This case was not going the way he wanted it to. Then he got a call from France. Interpol reported that two men had met at a café in Paris a few days ago. One of the men was a known as a fence of rare art objects. This was the tip Inspector Edwards was waiting for. Did Mr. Wellington get to France? He must have. The second man's height fit Mr. Wellington's description, but that was about all.

How did he get out of England with that Bible? Maybe it wasn't true that it was in a locker like William had suggested. Maybe Mr. Wellington had gotten it out some other way. That was of no matter now. What mattered was that Mr. Wellington was probably in France with the Bible, and it was out of Inspector Edwards' hands. He'd have to leave it up to the Interpol agents to find the man and then expedite his transfer back to England where he could stand trial for the murder of Mr. Harvard and the kidnapping of the Allen family.

Mr. Wellington made his way to Paris after arriving by boat from England. He went straight for the Hotel de Ville, where he planned to intercept the Bible. He got a room and told the desk clerk that he liked the hotel so much that he decided to come back on his holiday and stay there. That explanation was accepted without question. Mr. Wellington didn't mention the ash tray shipment. He figured he'd pay attention to the mail when it arrived and just snatch it. If anyone got in his way or gave him any trouble, he'd kill them and not give it another thought.

The package arrived; Mr. Wellington saw it being delivered. The bellboy took it and placed it in a back room, leaving it there until the manager could open it. The manager never got a chance to open it because Mr. Wellington worked quickly. He simply walked into the storeroom, took the package and walked out. No one saw him do it.

He went to his suite, opened the package, took out the Bible and put it into his suitcase. He called Pierre to make sure the coast was clear and then caught a cab for Pierre's apartment, which was not far from the Louvre. Pierre was waiting for him with the rare book expert.

The man was old, maybe 80, bald, and looked like he was going to die at any minute. He looked at the Bible briefly, but carefully, and said, "It's a Gutenberg all right!"

"Thank you professor," Pierre said. "I'll send you a check like agreed."

The professor left and Pierre said to Mr. Wellington, "Well, you got here in record time. How did you manage it?"

"No problem, I just moved quickly. Now what about my money?" Mr. Wellington asked.

"Give me a day or two, and I'll have it for you. I don't have 100,000,000 francs laying around in my apartment you know!" Pierre exclaimed.

"You said you'd have the money when I got here with the Bible; that was our deal," Mr. Wellington said.

"Yes, that's true, but I didn't expect you back so soon. You'll get your money; just be patient," Pierre responded.

"I'm not leaving the Bible here with you unless I stay here with it," Mr. Wellington replied.

"That's all been arranged. I told you I had a safe house for you to stay in until the deal was done, and that's what I'm going to do," Pierre said.

"I don't want to stay at your so-called safe house. How do I know it's safe? Besides I've paid good money for a suite at the Hotel de Ville! I'm going back there with the Bible and wait for your call," Mr. Wellington said as he turned on his heel, picked up the Bible and started for the door.

"Just stop right there, Francis," Pierre commanded.

Mr. Wellington turned and saw a gun in Pierre's hand.

"What's this all about?" Mr. Wellington asked.

"Just my insurance policy. You stay here," he said.

"So you're going to kill me and take the money for yourself. I thought we had an agreement, and we were old friends," Mr. Wellington said.

"We do have an agreement, and we are old friends. I would kill you and keep the Bible for myself, but because of our past friendship and all the money you've made for me, I'm going to honor my word – but you'll have to stay in my safe house like I planned or the whole deal is off. I can't afford to have you running all over Paris with that Bible, with every crook looking for you just to get their hands on the reward. You are worth more to me alive than dead," Pierre said.

"Thanks for your confidence in me," Mr. Wellington said. "OK, we'll do it your way, but what are they going to think when I don't return to my suite in the hotel?"

"They won't care. You came here to fish, remember, or so you told me over the phone, so they will think you went fishing," Pierre said.

"But all my fishing gear is in my room!" Mr. Wellington responded.

"Stop worrying about your fishing gear. I've got to get you to the safe house. Now are you going to cooperate, or do we do it the hard way?" Pierre asked.

So Mr. Wellington was taken to the safe house. It wasn't far from Pierre's place, somewhere on the west bank of the Seine River near Notre Dame Cathedral. The apartment, or room, was just that, a room with nothing in it except a chair and a bed. There was a sink and a toilet, but that's all. There wasn't even a refrigerator or a radio. Pierre drove him to a friend's house, who took him by car to the room. Mr. Wellington was left there with instructions not to go out anywhere for any reason. Food would be brought later, and he was just supposed to wait. Wait, but how long?

CHAPTER 10

Getting Caught

Nancy went to school at the St. Louis Convent in Newmarket, a small town near Soham. She was involved with the school's dance academy, which performed anywhere they were invited. Nancy was about to get the chance of her life by performing before Queen Elizabeth II. The queen was having a big party, and Nancy's school was asked to perform during the festivities. Nancy was beside herself with excitement.

When the time came for the big performance, Nancy was so wound up that she got sick. Fortunately, Mother pulled her through with a pep talk and a little ginger ale and saltine crackers. The performance went off like clockwork, and the crowd loved it. The queen herself even stood up to applaud at the end. This thrilled the dance troupe to no end.

After the program was over Mother, Nancy and I were invited to attend a reception to meet the queen, her husband, Prince Phillip, and the queen mother. The women in my family couldn't believe this was happening. They both had new dresses for the occasion. I was excited too, but for different reasons. I still had my arm in a cast and this was a bit embarrassing, but I'd get over it. After all, I was the hero who had had his picture in the London Times!

At the reception the queen mother asked Nancy's dance teacher if she would be willing to put together a group of other English school dance groups to perform in a combined program to be held at the Royal Opera House in Paris. What could she say except, yes, of course, she would be absolutely thrilled. The idea was the queen mother's herself. She thought it would be nice to have an arts exchange program with France. It was to be a good-will gesture by England. The whole thing was to take place in two weeks, so it was back to hours of daily rehearsals for the girls, only this time they would be dancing with four other schools in one combined program. The whole thing would be choreographed by Nancy's dance teacher. This was a great honor for her and the St. Louis Convent.

I didn't think it was fair that Nancy got to go to Paris but not me and Mother, so I called Inspector Edwards in London and told him so in no uncertain terms. He said he would make a few calls and see what he could do, and the next thing I knew Mother and I were invited to go along as guests of the queen mother. Before you could say "God bless the queen," we were on our way to Paris.

But we weren't the only ones on the move. Mr. Wellington finally had the money for the Bible. By anyone's standards he was now a rich man. He was eager to get out of Paris and head to Argentina, but there was just one problem. He needed a new identity and a new passport. This would take time and money, but he didn't want to risk getting caught at this point. The word on the streets of Paris was that he was still hot – Bible or no Bible.

Pierre had told him he knew someone who would do the passport, but it would cost a pretty penny because he was so hot. Mr. Wellington was not going to be able to kill this guy because Pierre knew him. The passport forger was a personal friend of Pierre's and if anything happened to the man Pierre assured Mr. Wellington that he would never leave France.

The contact was made and the appointment set. Mr. Wellington met the man at a little apartment not far from the safe house, where he continued to stay. The man was cautious when letting Mr. Wellington inside his apartment. He had to use a password and come alone. Mr. Wellington complied.

When Mr. Wellington entered the apartment, the smell of cleaning fluid was overwhelming. A small man of maybe 50 years old greeted him and asked him to sit down. The apartment was old, cold and something of a dump. The furniture was ripped and torn, and the place looked like it hadn't been cleaned since the war.

"I'm Phillipé," the man said in a rather feminine voice. "Won't you be seated? Pierre has told me that you need a new identity and a new passport, is that true?"

"Yes," Mr. Wellington said.

"Tell me, ah, Francis, is that your name?" Phillipé asked.

"Not for long," Mr. Wellington responded. "I need a new name, a new look and a new passport to go with it."

"That is what I'm here for," Phillipé said. "First we are going to have to do something about that scar on your face. I suggest a beard; yes, that would do nicely. Maybe a light gray to go with your hair? I think you would look better older, maybe even walking with a cane. Older people are not suspected as much by the police as younger people."

"Whatever you think is best. What is all this going to cost?" Mr. Wellington asked.

"For you, a friend of Pierre, I think 1,000,000 francs would be in order," Phillipé said.

"One million francs! You must be crazy!" Mr. Wellington exclaimed.

"This is my discount rate. Remember, you are the most wanted man in France and England right now and…" Phillipé said.

"And you're going to take advantage of that," Mr. Wellington interrupted.

"Instead of 'take advantage' I'd say it is your only choice at this point," Phillipé responded.

"How long will it take?" Mr. Wellington asked.

"Well, *mon ami*, let's say a few weeks for you to grow a beard and…" Phillipé started to say.

"A few weeks for me to grow a beard? Why not use a fake beard?" Mr. Wellington inquired.

"I could do that, but it would not be as authentic," Phillipé replied.

"Let's go with the fake beard – how long?" Mr. Wellington asked.

"Well, with a fake beard, hair dye, age wrinkles and the new passport, maybe two weeks," was the answer.

"Two weeks? Are you kidding?" Mr. Wellington asked in surprise.

"Do you want the job done right or don't you?" Phillipé questioned.

"All right, all right, you've got a deal. When can we get started?" Mr. Wellington asked.

"Oh, right away, right away," Phillipé assured him. "I'll just need half the payment now and the rest when I'm done."

"I'll get the money for you tomorrow. I'll meet you here at nine o' clock in the morning, OK?" Mr. Wellington said.

"Make it two in the afternoon; I have some other business to conduct in the morning," Phillipé said.

"Two in the afternoon it is," Mr. Wellington replied.

"Make sure it is all in cash, Please," Phillipé requested.

Meanwhile, Inspector Edwards needed to go to Paris to meet with his Interpol contact. He suggested that he accompany my family to France since Father was unable to. Mother accepted his offer since it was Inspector Edwards who smoothed the way for us to go. How he did that, he never said, and I didn't ask him either.

Our flight to Paris was a short one. We landed at Le Bourget Airfield at night. Inspector Edwards had everything worked out for us, even the hotel – the Hotel de Ville. The rooms were small. Mother and Nancy stayed in one room and Inspector Edwards and I stayed in another. There was a television set in the room, but everything was in French so I couldn't follow anything I turned on. "The Roy Rogers Show" was on, but it was in French and Roy didn't sound like Roy to me! The lip sync wasn't right either.

While Mother and Nancy went to rehearsals, Inspector Edwards and I went to see his contact at Interpol. When we got to the Interpol office, we were greeted by a woman who had her hair tied up in a bun like Mrs. Wallis, the postmistress in Soham. This lady was all business. She told us to follow her, which we did. She walked fast, practically running up the stairs to the second floor. She led us to an office door that said Foreign Affairs on it. She took us in and said to be seated.

"Capt. Yarris will be out in a moment" she said.

Then she spun around and marched out like she had been on parade in the Air Force. A couple of minutes later a very tall man came through the door wearing a plain gray suit, vest, tie and black shoes. He looked like he was about Father's age.

"Good morning Inspector," he said as he put out his hand to shake Inspector Edwards' hand. "And this must be the famous William Allen you have been telling me about."

"Hi!" I said.

"Inspector Edwards tells me that you solved the crime of who stole the Gutenberg Bible and killed Mr. Cox," Capt. Yarris said.

"Yes sir," I said.

"Well, it's a pleasure to have you here. Welcome to Interpol," he replied.

He invited us into his office for some tea. His office was not big, but it was well furnished with leather chairs, a matching leather sofa and a beautiful coffee table made of mahogany. There was a sterling silver tea set on the table with hot tea and some delicious cakes. We drank tea and ate cake while Inspector Edwards and Capt. Yarris talked about Mr. Wellington. It seemed that Mr. Wellington was in Paris according to the latest information Capt. Yarris had received from his contacts. Where he was and what he was doing was anyone's guess.

"Do you mind if I comment on the situation?" I asked.

"Be my guest William," Capt. Yarris said.

"Well, if I were Mr. Wellington the first thing I would do is sell the Bible to the highest bidder and then get out of Dodge as fast as I could," I said.

"Get out of Dodge? Excuse me William, but what does that mean, get out of Dodge?" Capt. Yarris inquired.

"It means get out of town, and fast," I explained. "If Mr. Wellington has already sold the Bible, which I bet he has, then he needs to change his identity and skip the country as fast as he can without being caught. If I were him I'd go someplace where no one could find me."

"And where would that be?" Inspector Edwards asked.

"I don't know, but I sure wouldn't go back to England or stay here," I said.

"That makes sense Inspector," Capt. Yarris said. "We have also suspected that Mr. Wellington, or whatever his name is, has probably already sold the Bible and would be looking for a way to escape the country without be detected. My men are on the lookout right now for any known passport makers, of the unlawful type, and they are to get information to me as soon as possible. I have some money floating around out there so snitches can turn in information to me. You understand, William?"

"Yes, I do, but I wouldn't wait very long because I bet he's trying to get out fast, especially if he's already got the money. If this guy is really German like we think, then maybe he'll go back to Germany where he has family and they can hide him," I suggested.

"That's a possibility," the inspector said.

"On the other hand," I continued, "what if he doesn't have any family in Germany, then where would he go?"

"Most Germans went home after the war, but some, especially those who were accused of war crimes or were secret agents, tried to escape to other countries," Capt. Yarris said.

"Like what other countries?" I asked.

"Well, a lot of Germans went to Argentina after the war. They had sent money there, and Argentina and Bolivia accepted them with open arms. Most other countries would not accept Germans after the war, but some would, like Switzerland and Austria," Capt. Yarris explained.

"But why Argentina and Bolivia? Aren't they a long way from Germany?" I asked.

"Yes they are, but money talks and when people are paid large sums of money to keep their mouth shut, then that's what they do," Inspector Edwards said.

"But you've given me an idea, William," Capt. Yarris said. "If indeed Mr. Wellington is trying to get to South America, then we need to be watching all the flights and ships leaving France."

He pressed a button on a box on his desk.

"Miss Rochet, would you come in here please?" he said into the box, which must have been an intercom.

The door opened almost immediately and in walked the lady who led us into the office. She marched in and said, "Yes, sir," just like they do in the military.

"Miss Rochet, please advise the radio operator to alert the airports and ports on the coast to be on the lookout for our suspect traveling to South America. Also, send that artist picture along to each station chief," he ordered.

"Yes, sir," she said and marched out of the office.

"Our next step, Inspector, is to track down every possible illegal passport forger in Paris. We have a list of most of them and already have their places of business staked out," Capt. Yarris said.

"I've got to go Inspector. The performance is tomorrow night, but there is a dress rehearsal tonight and Mother wants me there," I said.

"Yes, William, you're quite right, quite right. Please excuse us, Captain. We have to go, but I'll be in touch with later," Inspector Edwards said.

"Good luck, William," Capt. Yarris said.

We left Interpol and stopped at a sidewalk café for tea and a snack before we headed back to the hotel. There are sidewalk cafés all over Paris; the one we picked was very crowded. There was one table open, and we took it quickly before anyone else could get it. Inspector Edwards ordered some tea and little tea cakes. We were surrounded by all sorts of people speaking in French, of course; they all fascinated me so I listened intently even though I didn't understand what they were saying. Our tea and cakes arrived and we had begun eating when I heard a familiar voice from a table behind us. I didn't need a fish smell to recognize that voice; I'd know it anywhere. It was Mr. Wellington. I was sure of it!

"Inspector, don't look around, but I think I hear Mr. Wellington's voice behind us," I said quietly.

"Are you sure?" the inspector inquired.

"Yes, I'm sure. It's him I tell you; I know his voice," I said excitedly.

Inspector Edwards decided to head to the restroom as an excuse for trying to spot Mr. Wellington. He told me to sit still and stay put. He slipped out of his seat casually and walked away toward the restrooms. He hoped that the crowd would cover his limp and Mr. Wellington would not notice him. His plan worked. When he got to the other side of the café he peeked around a post and surveyed the crowd. Inspector

Edwards recognized Mr. Wellington despite his disguise. He was dressed in a business suit, had brown hair and a handlebar moustache.

Mr. Wellington had not had time to change his looks yet. He was still waiting for Phillipé to make the gray wig and beard. He couldn't grow one because it would come in black, so a beard of real gray hair had to be constructed.

All this was taking too much time, Mr. Wellington thought, but he still had to eat. He was told not to leave his room, but he was getting stir crazy in there and he needed some fresh air. What could a little time in a crowded café hurt?

Inspector Edwards got on the phone to Capt. Yaris immediately. He in turn sent police to the café. Inspector Edwards returned to our table and told me to just act naturally and not to look around. He said the police would be there any minute. He would not have to act unless Mr. Wellington left before the police got there. Inspector Edwards had a gun, which was unusual for Scotland Yard personnel, but Capt. Yarris had slipped it to him when I wasn't looking.

"I don't want to use this unless there is no other way," he said to me.

"How will the police know which one is Mr. Wellington?" I asked.

"I described him to Capt. Yarris in detail, and even described where he is sitting. I also said he was alone and possibly armed," the inspector said.

We waited for what seemed a long time, but it really wasn't. The French police showed up and tore through the café to Mr. Wellington's table. They came from everywhere at once. They pounced on Mr. Wellington before he had a chance to run. He was handcuffed and led toward our table. Inspector Edwards stood up just as Mr. Wellington got to our table.

"Well, well. We meet again, Mr. Wellington. Only this time I have the gun, and you are the prisoner who can't get away. Young William here heard your voice ordering from the waiter, and that's all he needed to identify you," Inspector Edwards said.

"So it's you again!" Mr. Wellington said, looking right at me. "You little brat! I'll get even with you if it's the last thing I ever do."

"Take him away," Inspector Edwards said the police. "Don't worry, William. He'll be extradited to England, stand trial and be put away for the rest of his life. He'll never bother you or your family ever again."

I went to Nancy's performance the next night with a feeling of joy and relief. Mother was relieved and couldn't believe that I had helped catch Mr. Wellington. Again my picture was in the paper, only this time it was in a French paper: "Nine-year-old William Allen captures international criminal" was the headline.

I didn't really capture Mr. Wellington – it was the French police – but it sure sounded good to me. Inspector Edwards talked to Father in England, and he said the story was on the front page of all the British papers, too. I wondered if Billy saw it.

The Gutenberg Bible was found in the possession of one Pierre la Foote. Mr. Wellington confessed that he had sold it to him and the French authorities picked Mr. La Foote up quickly. He still had the Bible, so it was shipped by special courier to England where it now is prominently displayed in the Museum of Natural History in London. My family had our picture taken with Inspector Edwards and the Gutenberg Bible. Father was not in the picture, of course, because he had some important business to do for the Air Force at the time the picture was made.

My life returned to normal, with school and our daily routines. My celebrity status didn't last long, but it was fun while it did last. I was interviewed by everybody from the British tabloids to American magazines. My arm healed and the cast was removed. Nancy returned to St. Louis Convent in Newmarket.

Mother still made me toast with jelly and hot chocolate when I came home from school, and she still put Freddy in my window so I could see him when I walked up our driveway in Soham. The church bells still woke me up every morning, but now they were rung by a new assistant to Rev. Holder. The spiders still clung to the ceiling in my closet bedroom, but they didn't seem to bother me like they used to. I was a lot older now, and braver; I was almost 10.

About the Author

An educator for more than 42 years, author Duane C. Burritt has taught elementary school, middle school, high school and college. He received a bachelor's degree in elementary education and two master's degrees in educational administration and elementary education. Mr. Burritt also received a doctorate in Christian education and served as principal of a K-12 Christian school he started in Pensacola, Florida.

For nine years, Mr. Burritt served as an assistant professor in the education department at Oral Roberts University (ORU) where he published several articles and a science experiment textbook; during his tenure at ORU he frequently spoke at education conferences.

Clearly, the father of two sons and three grandchildren has given his life to investing in the lives of young people. In authoring his first children's book, Mr. Burritt hopes to capture the curiosity and stir the imaginations of children everywhere.

Mr. Burritt and his wife, Linda, make their home in T'' Oklahoma.

CPSIA information can be obtained at www.ICGtesting.com
235403LV00001B/11/P

9 780984 067374